STONE ARCH BOOKS
a capstone imprint

THE BATMAN STRIKES!®

STONE ARCH BOOKS™

Published in 2015 by Stone Arch Books
A Capstone Imprint
1710 Roe Crest Drive
North Mankato, MN 56003
www.capstonepub.com

Originally published by DC Comics in the U.S. in single magazine form as The Batman Strikes! #11.

DC Comics
1700 Broadway, New York, NY 10019
A Warner Bros. Entertainment Company

Printed in China by Nordica.
0914/CA21401510
092014 008470NORDS15

Cataloging-in-Publication Data is available at the Library of Congress website.
ISBN: 978-1-4342-9664-1 (library binding)

Summary: Penguin has Batman on the ropes, and only Alfred can save him. Will this strange dynamic duo be able to protect Gotham City?

STONE ARCH BOOKS
Ashley C. Andersen Zantop *Publisher*
Michael Dahl *Editorial Director*
Eliza Leahy *Editor*
Heather Kindseth *Creative Director*
Peggie Carley *Designer*
Tori Abraham *Production Specialist*

DC COMICS
Nachie Castro *Original U.S. Editor*

ALFRED
TO THE
RESCUE?!

BILL MATHENY ....WRITER

CHRISTOPHER JONES ....PENCILLER

TERRY BEATTY...INKER

HEROIC AGE...COLORIST

PHIL BALSMAN...LETTERER

BATMAN CREATED BY
BOB KANE

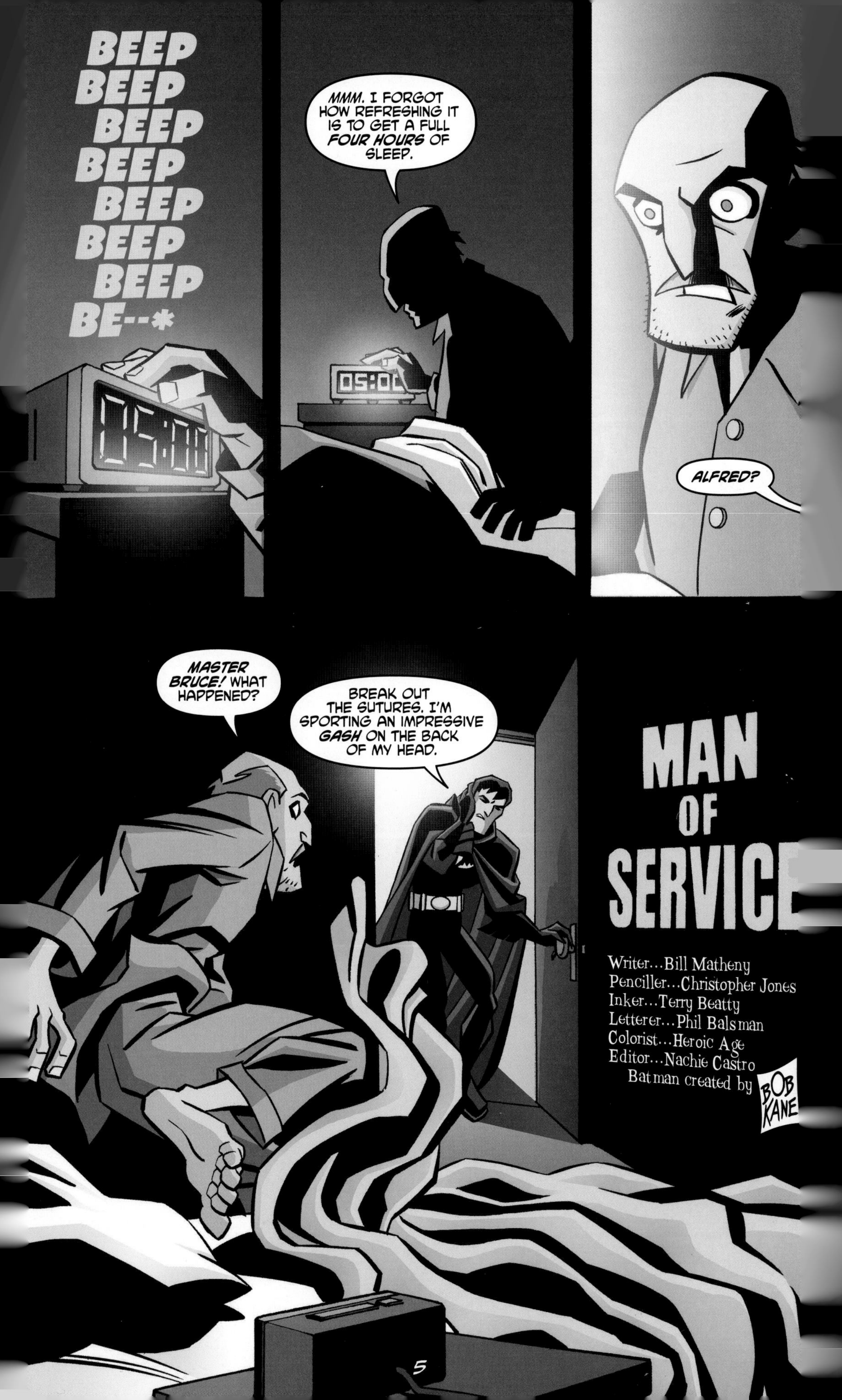
BEEP
BEEP
BEEP
BEEP
BEEP
BEEP
BEEP
BE--*
MMM. I FORGOT HOW REFRESHING IT IS TO GET A FULL FOUR HOURS OF SLEEP.
ALFRED?
MASTER BRUCE! WHAT HAPPENED?
BREAK OUT THE SUTURES. I'M SPORTING AN IMPRESSIVE GASH ON THE BACK OF MY HEAD.
MAN OF SERVICE
Writer...Bill Matheny
Penciller...Christopher Jones
Inker...Terry Beatty
Letterer...Phil Balsman
Colorist...Heroic Age
Editor...Nachie Castro
Batman created by BOB KANE

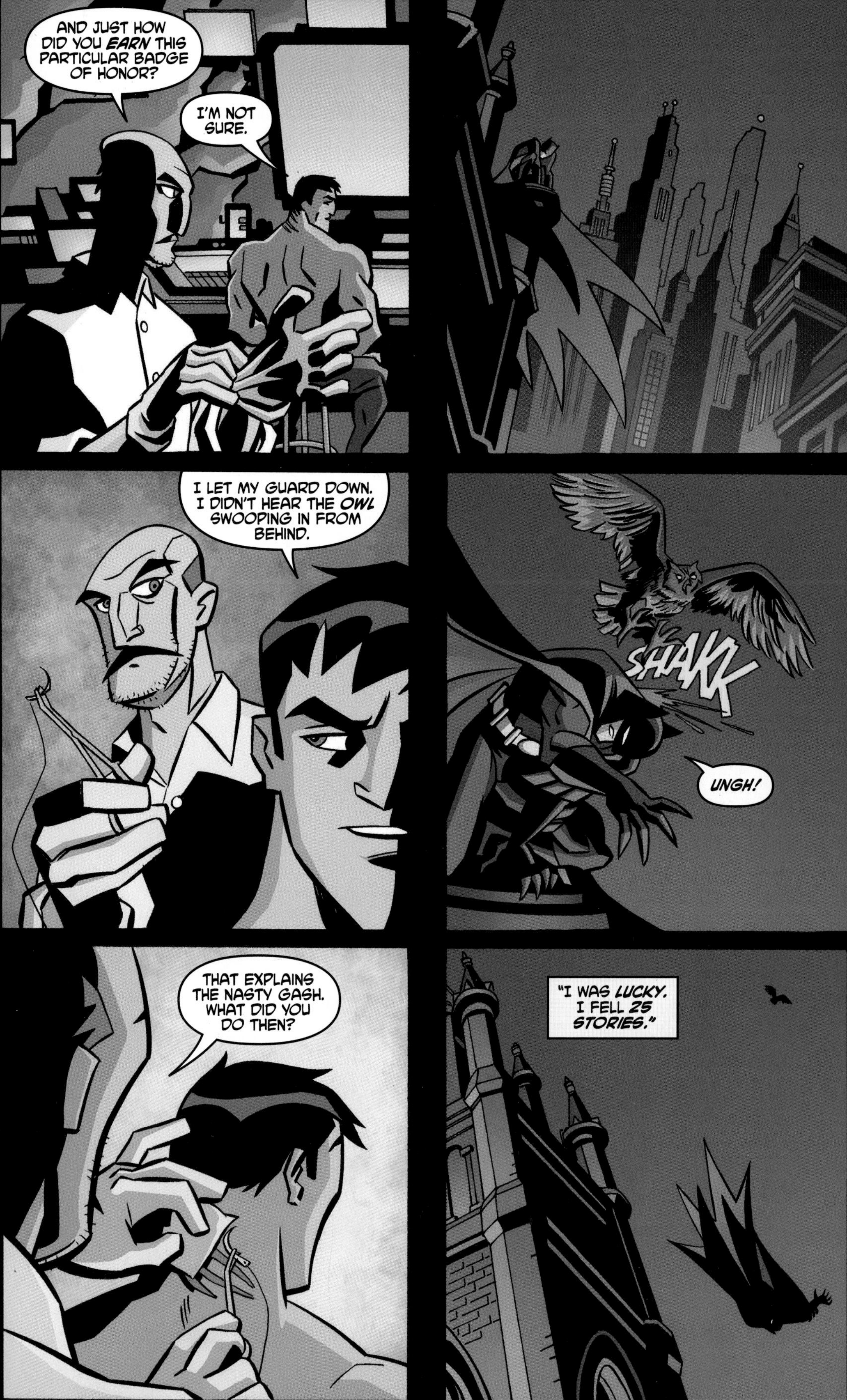
AND JUST HOW DID YOU EARN THIS PARTICULAR BADGE OF HONOR?
I'M NOT SURE.
I LET MY GUARD DOWN. I DIDN'T HEAR THE OWL SWOOPING IN FROM BEHIND.
SHAKK
UNGH!
THAT EXPLAINS THE NASTY GASH. WHAT DID YOU DO THEN?
"I WAS LUCKY. I FELL 25 STORIES."

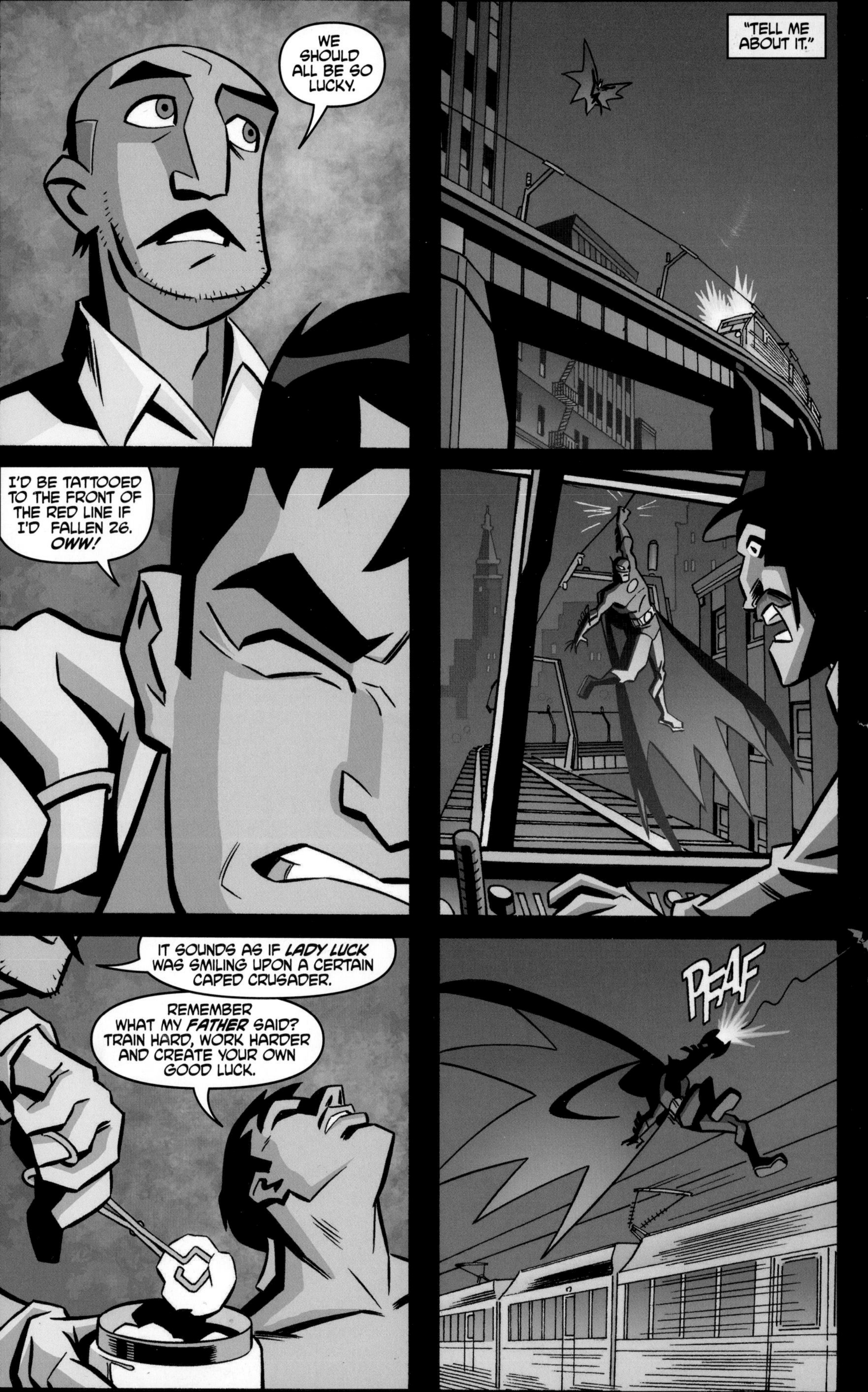
WE SHOULD ALL BE SO LUCKY.
"TELL ME ABOUT IT."
I'D BE TATTOOED TO THE FRONT OF THE RED LINE IF I'D FALLEN 26. OWW!
IT SOUNDS AS IF LADY LUCK WAS SMILING UPON A CERTAIN CAPED CRUSADER.
REMEMBER WHAT MY FATHER SAID? TRAIN HARD, WORK HARDER AND CREATE YOUR OWN GOOD LUCK.
PFAF

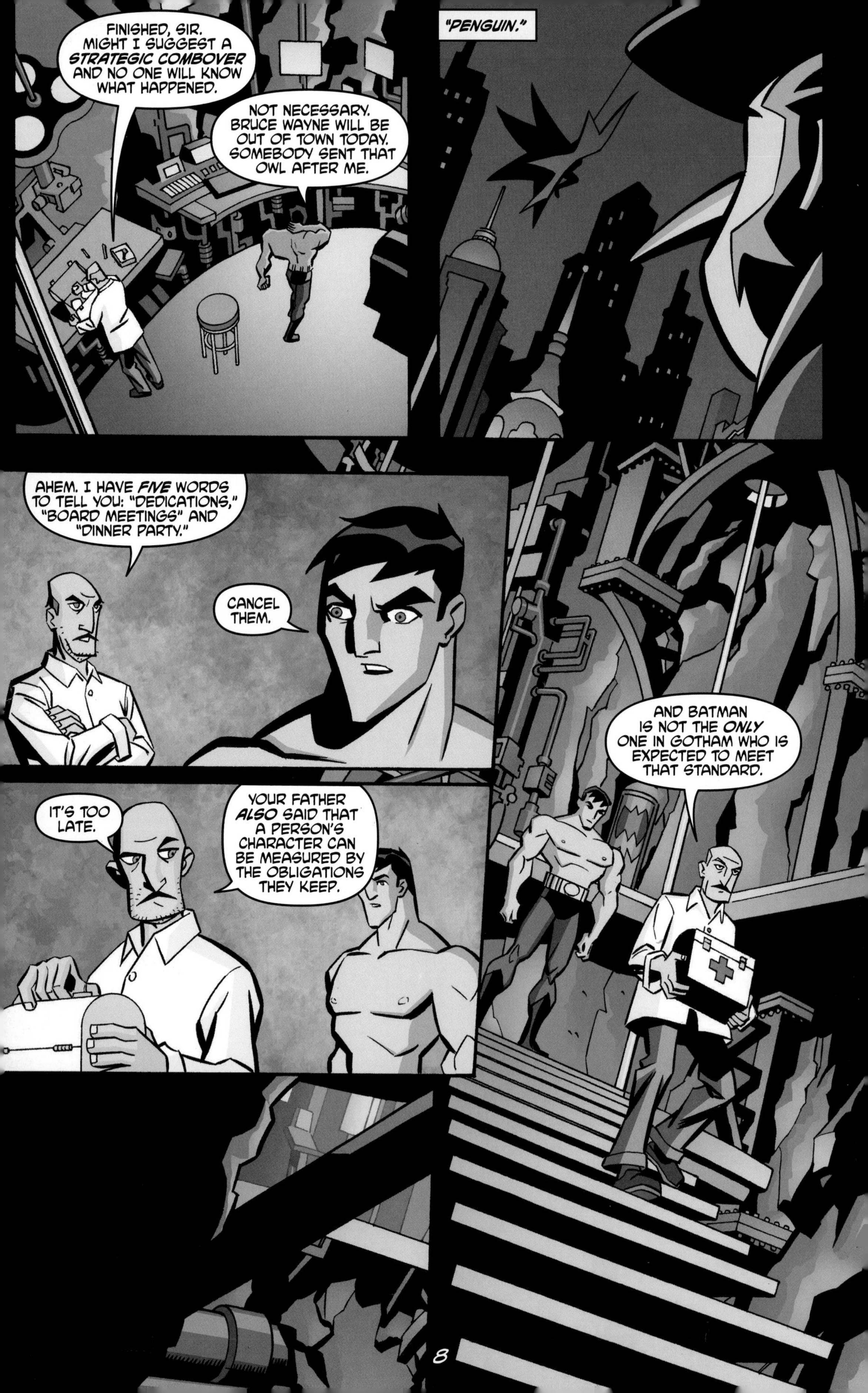
FINISHED, SIR. MIGHT I SUGGEST A STRATEGIC COMBOVER AND NO ONE WILL KNOW WHAT HAPPENED.
NOT NECESSARY. BRUCE WAYNE WILL BE OUT OF TOWN TODAY. SOMEBODY SENT THAT OWL AFTER ME.
"PENGUIN."
AHEM. I HAVE FIVE WORDS TO TELL YOU: "DEDICATIONS," "BOARD MEETINGS" AND "DINNER PARTY."
CANCEL THEM.
IT'S TOO LATE.
YOUR FATHER ALSO SAID THAT A PERSON'S CHARACTER CAN BE MEASURED BY THE OBLIGATIONS THEY KEEP.
AND BATMAN IS NOT THE ONLY ONE IN GOTHAM WHO IS EXPECTED TO MEET THAT STANDARD.

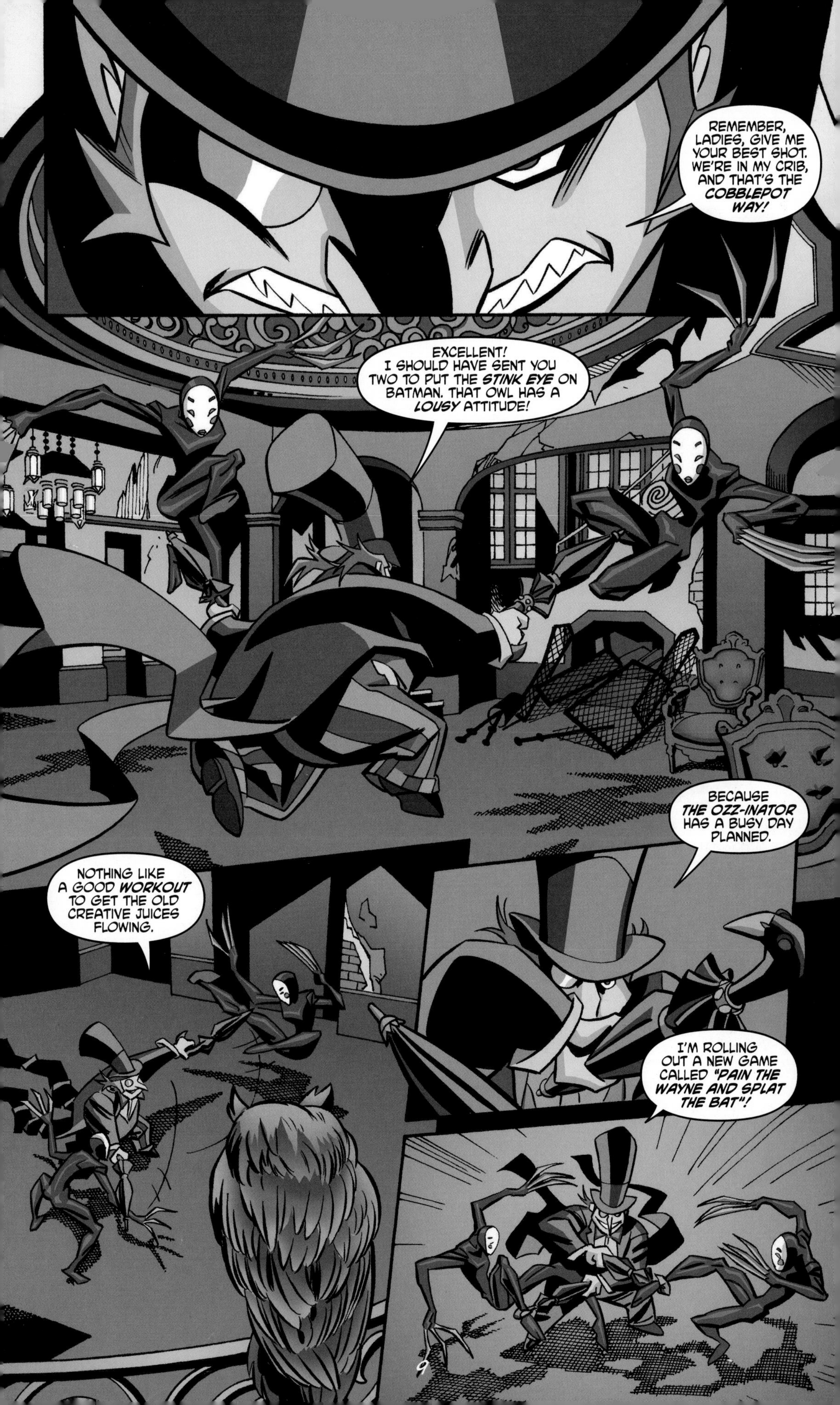
REMEMBER, LADIES, GIVE ME YOUR BEST SHOT. WE'RE IN MY CRIB, AND THAT'S THE COBBLEPOT WAY!
EXCELLENT! I SHOULD HAVE SENT YOU TWO TO PUT THE STINK EYE ON BATMAN. THAT OWL HAS A LOUSY ATTITUDE!
BECAUSE THE OZZ-INATOR HAS A BUSY DAY PLANNED.
NOTHING LIKE A GOOD WORKOUT TO GET THE OLD CREATIVE JUICES FLOWING.
I'M ROLLING OUT A NEW GAME CALLED "PAIN THE WAYNE AND SPLAT THE BAT"!

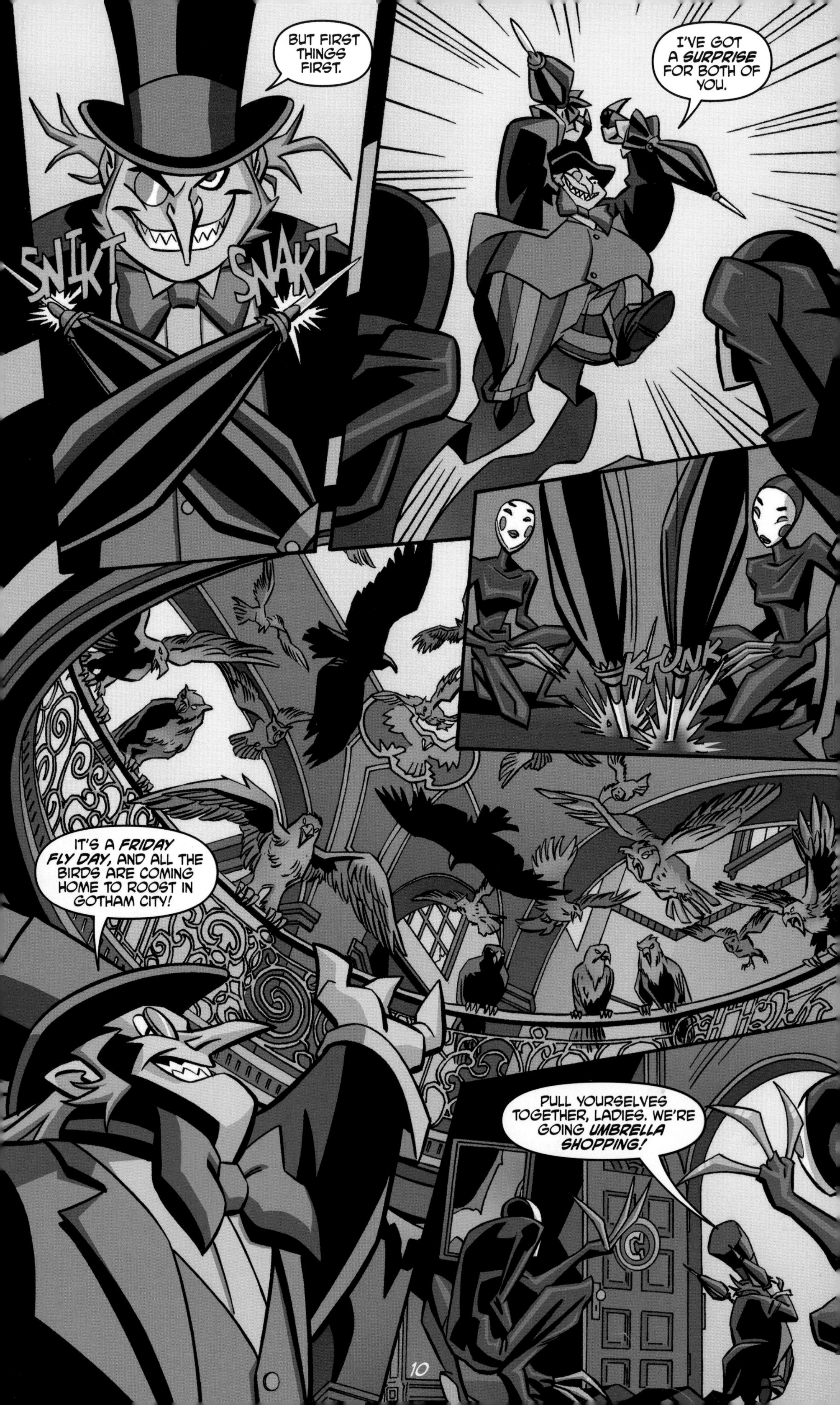

BUT FIRST THINGS FIRST.
SNIKT
SNAKT
I'VE GOT A SURPRISE FOR BOTH OF YOU.
KTUNK
IT'S A FRIDAY FLY DAY, AND ALL THE BIRDS ARE COMING HOME TO ROOST IN GOTHAM CITY!
PULL YOURSELVES TOGETHER, LADIES. WE'RE GOING UMBRELLA SHOPPING!

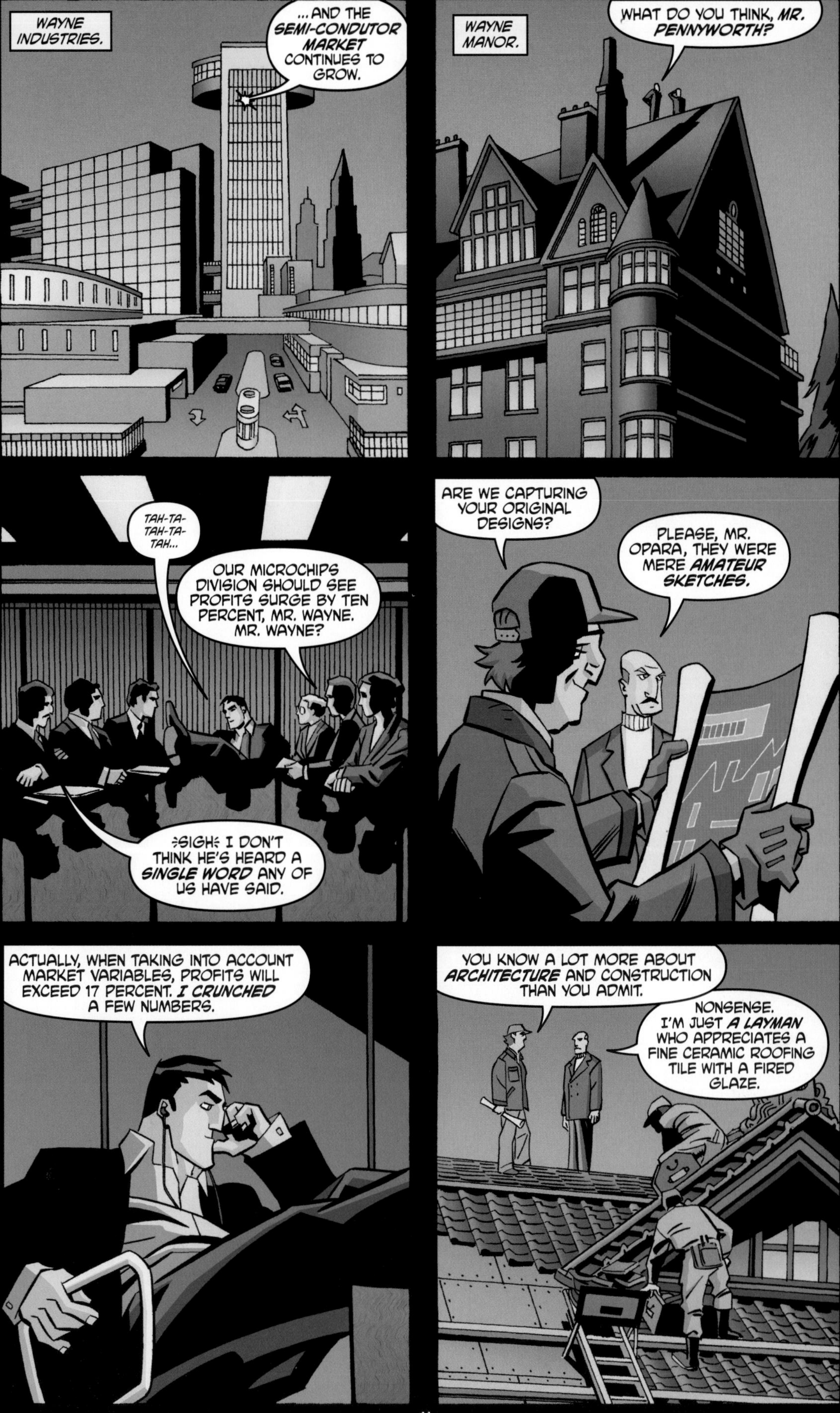

WAYNE INDUSTRIES.
...AND THE SEMI-CONDUTOR MARKET CONTINUES TO GROW.
WAYNE MANOR.
WHAT DO YOU THINK, MR. PENNYWORTH?
TAH-TA-TAH-TA-TAH...
OUR MICROCHIPS DIVISION SHOULD SEE PROFITS SURGE BY TEN PERCENT, MR. WAYNE. MR. WAYNE?
SIGH I DON'T THINK HE'S HEARD A SINGLE WORD ANY OF US HAVE SAID.
ARE WE CAPTURING YOUR ORIGINAL DESIGNS?
PLEASE, MR. OPARA, THEY WERE MERE AMATEUR SKETCHES.
ACTUALLY, WHEN TAKING INTO ACCOUNT MARKET VARIABLES, PROFITS WILL EXCEED 17 PERCENT. I CRUNCHED A FEW NUMBERS.
YOU KNOW A LOT MORE ABOUT ARCHITECTURE AND CONSTRUCTION THAN YOU ADMIT.
NONSENSE. I'M JUST A LAYMAN WHO APPRECIATES A FINE CERAMIC ROOFING TILE WITH A FIRED GLAZE.

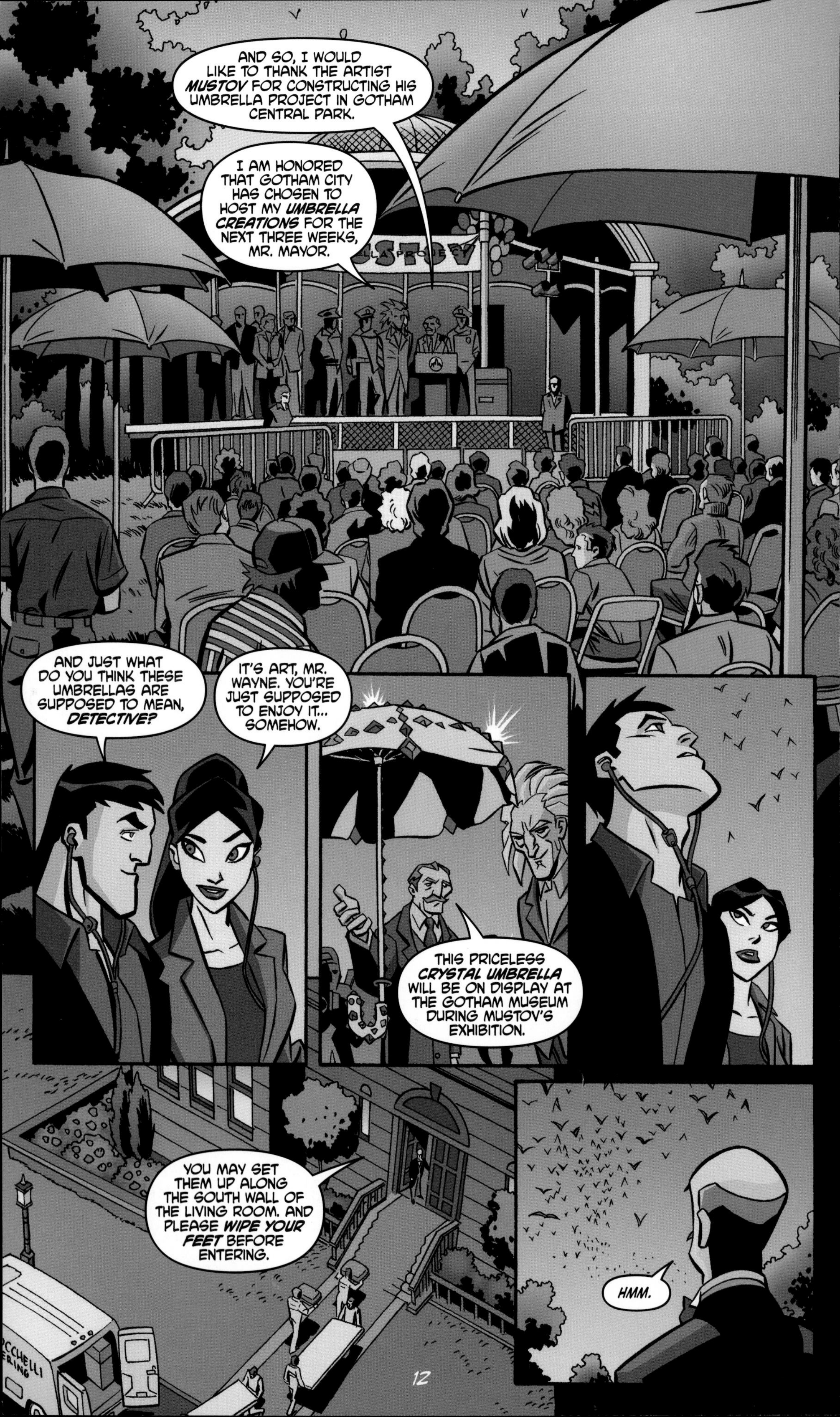
AND SO, I WOULD LIKE TO THANK THE ARTIST MUSTOV FOR CONSTRUCTING HIS UMBRELLA PROJECT IN GOTHAM CENTRAL PARK.
I AM HONORED THAT GOTHAM CITY HAS CHOSEN TO HOST MY UMBRELLA CREATIONS FOR THE NEXT THREE WEEKS, MR. MAYOR.
AND JUST WHAT DO YOU THINK THESE UMBRELLAS ARE SUPPOSED TO MEAN, DETECTIVE?
IT'S ART, MR. WAYNE. YOU'RE JUST SUPPOSED TO ENJOY IT... SOMEHOW.
THIS PRICELESS CRYSTAL UMBRELLA WILL BE ON DISPLAY AT THE GOTHAM MUSEUM DURING MUSTOV'S EXHIBITION.
YOU MAY SET THEM UP ALONG THE SOUTH WALL OF THE LIVING ROOM. AND PLEASE WIPE YOUR FEET BEFORE ENTERING.
HMM.

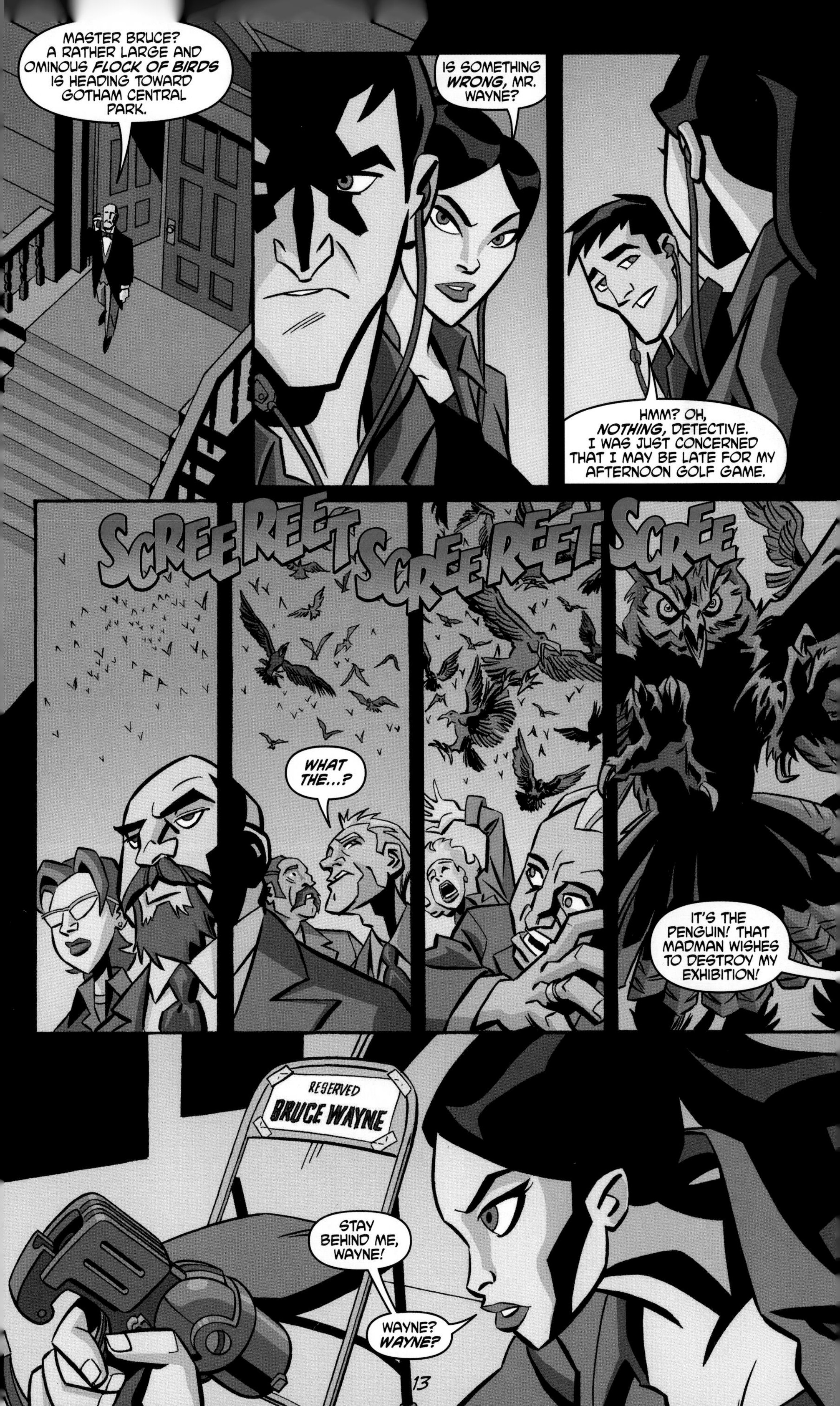
MASTER BRUCE? A RATHER LARGE AND OMINOUS FLOCK OF BIRDS IS HEADING TOWARD GOTHAM CENTRAL PARK.
IS SOMETHING WRONG, MR. WAYNE?
HMM? OH, NOTHING, DETECTIVE. I WAS JUST CONCERNED THAT I MAY BE LATE FOR MY AFTERNOON GOLF GAME.
SCREE REET SCREE REET SCREE
WHAT THE...?
IT'S THE PENGUIN! THAT MADMAN WISHES TO DESTROY MY EXHIBITION!
RESERVED
BRUCE WAYNE
STAY BEHIND ME, WAYNE!
WAYNE? WAYNE?

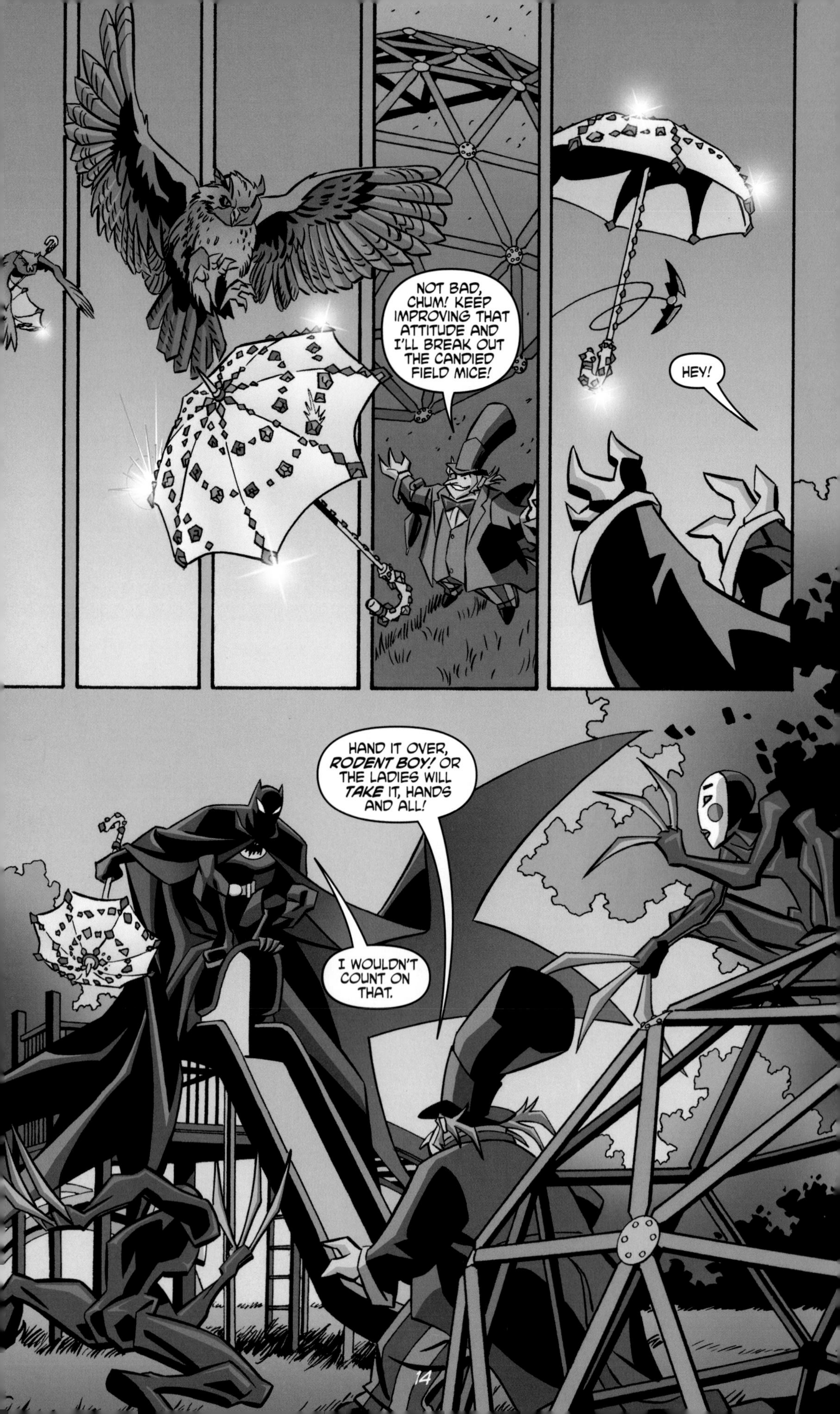
NOT BAD, CHUM! KEEP IMPROVING THAT ATTITUDE AND I'LL BREAK OUT THE CANDIED FIELD MICE!
HEY!
HAND IT OVER, *RODENT BOY!* OR THE LADIES WILL *TAKE* IT, HANDS AND ALL!
I WOULDN'T COUNT ON THAT.

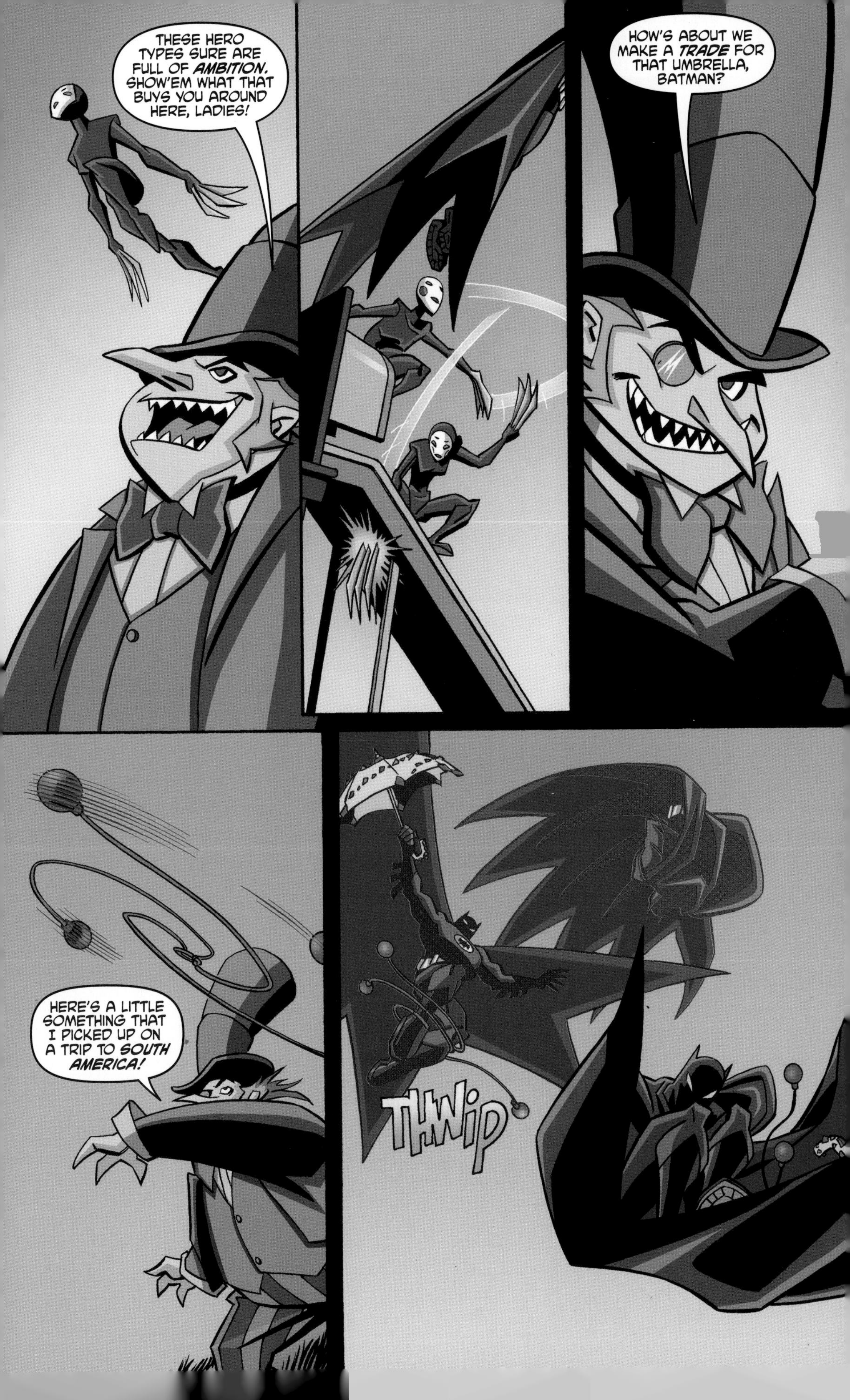

THESE HERO TYPES SURE ARE FULL OF *AMBITION.* SHOW'EM WHAT THAT BUYS YOU AROUND HERE, LADIES!
HOW'S ABOUT WE MAKE A *TRADE* FOR THAT UMBRELLA, BATMAN?
HERE'S A LITTLE SOMETHING THAT I PICKED UP ON A TRIP TO *SOUTH AMERICA!*
THWIP

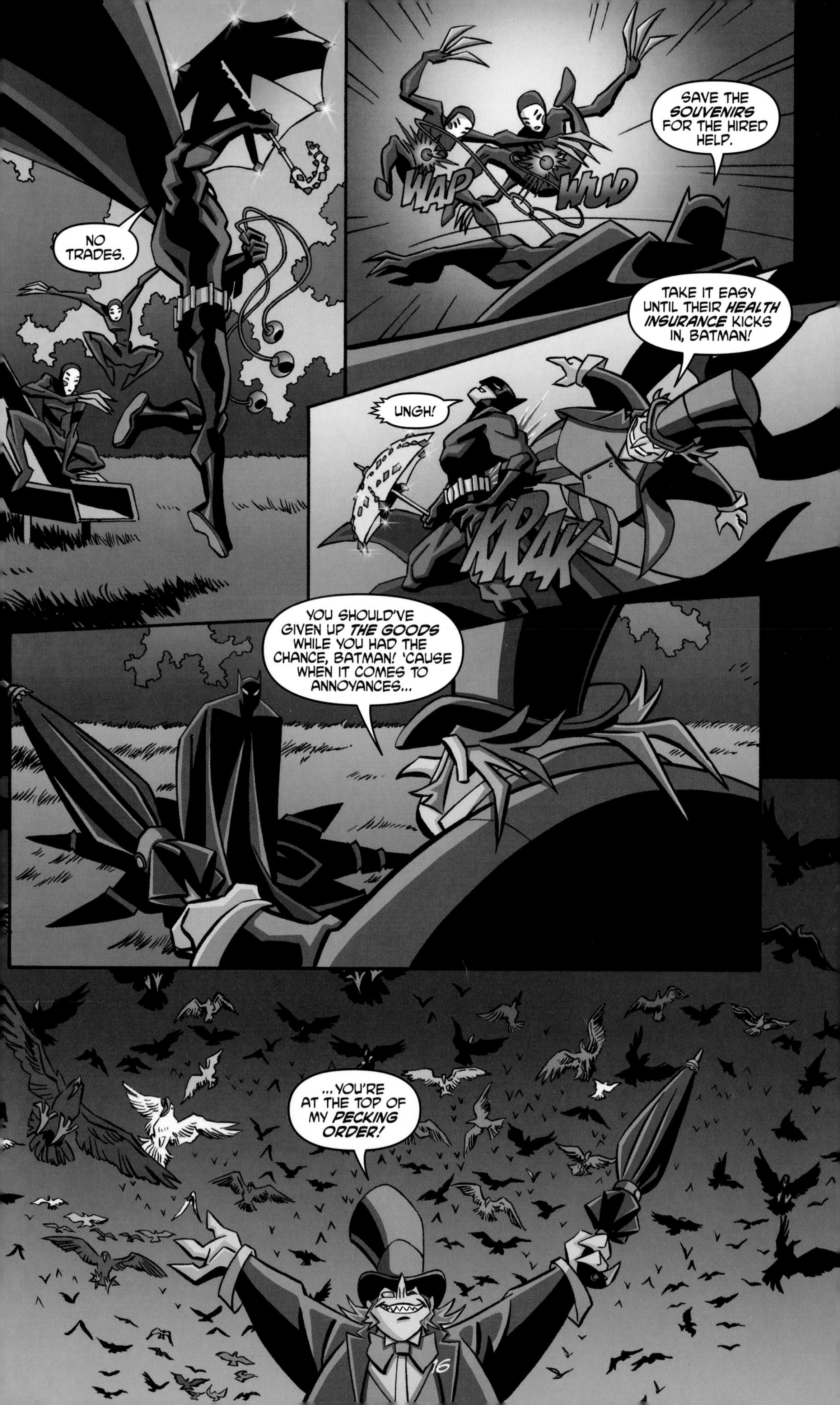
NO TRADES.
WAP
WUD
SAVE THE SOUVENIRS FOR THE HIRED HELP.
TAKE IT EASY UNTIL THEIR HEALTH INSURANCE KICKS IN, BATMAN!
UNGH!
KRAK
YOU SHOULD'VE GIVEN UP THE GOODS WHILE YOU HAD THE CHANCE, BATMAN! 'CAUSE WHEN IT COMES TO ANNOYANCES...
...YOU'RE AT THE TOP OF MY PECKING ORDER!

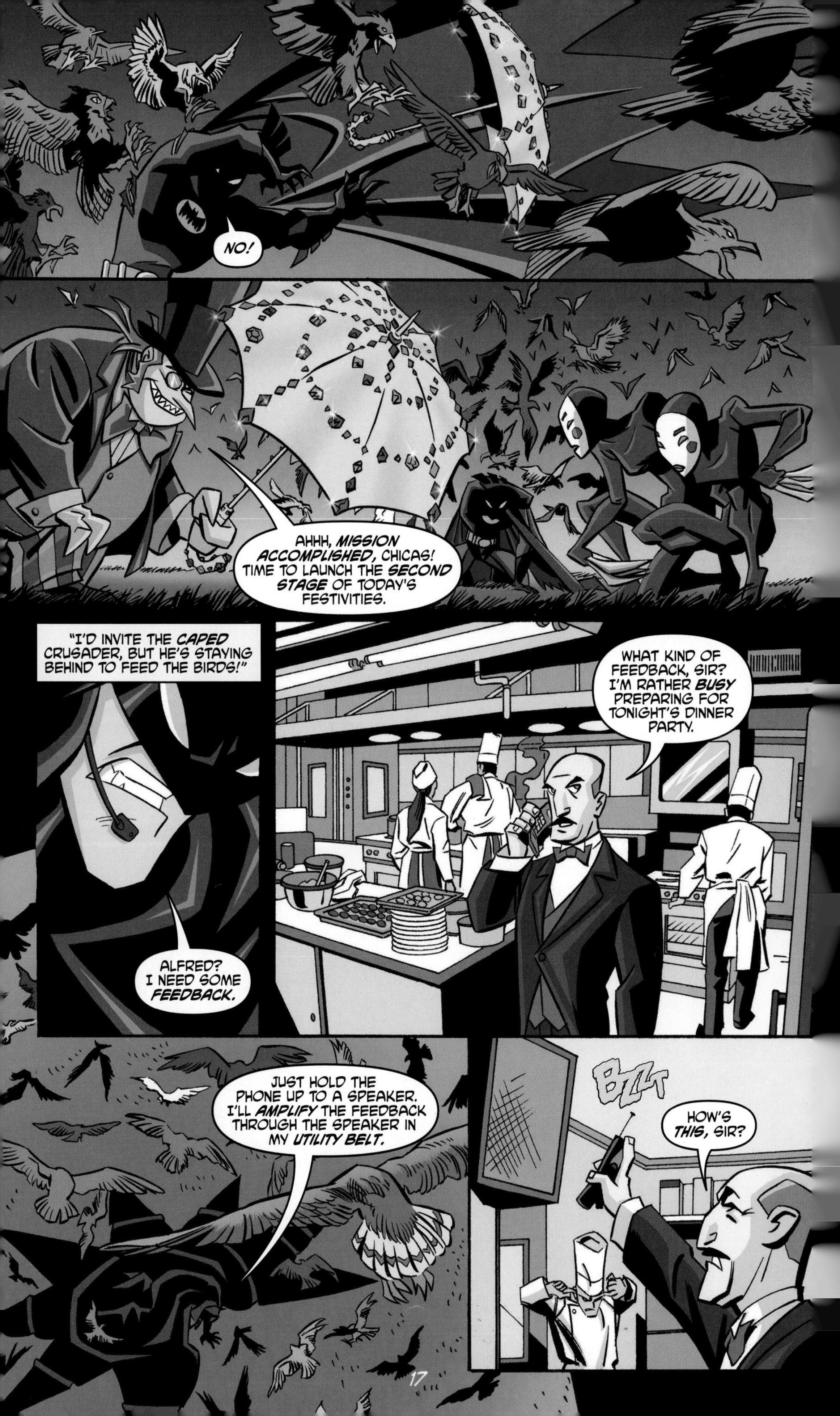
NO!
AHHH, MISSION ACCOMPLISHED, CHICAS! TIME TO LAUNCH THE SECOND STAGE OF TODAY'S FESTIVITIES.
"I'D INVITE THE CAPED CRUSADER, BUT HE'S STAYING BEHIND TO FEED THE BIRDS!"
ALFRED? I NEED SOME FEEDBACK.
WHAT KIND OF FEEDBACK, SIR? I'M RATHER BUSY PREPARING FOR TONIGHT'S DINNER PARTY.
JUST HOLD THE PHONE UP TO A SPEAKER. I'LL AMPLIFY THE FEEDBACK THROUGH THE SPEAKER IN MY UTILITY BELT.
BZZZT
HOW'S THIS, SIR?

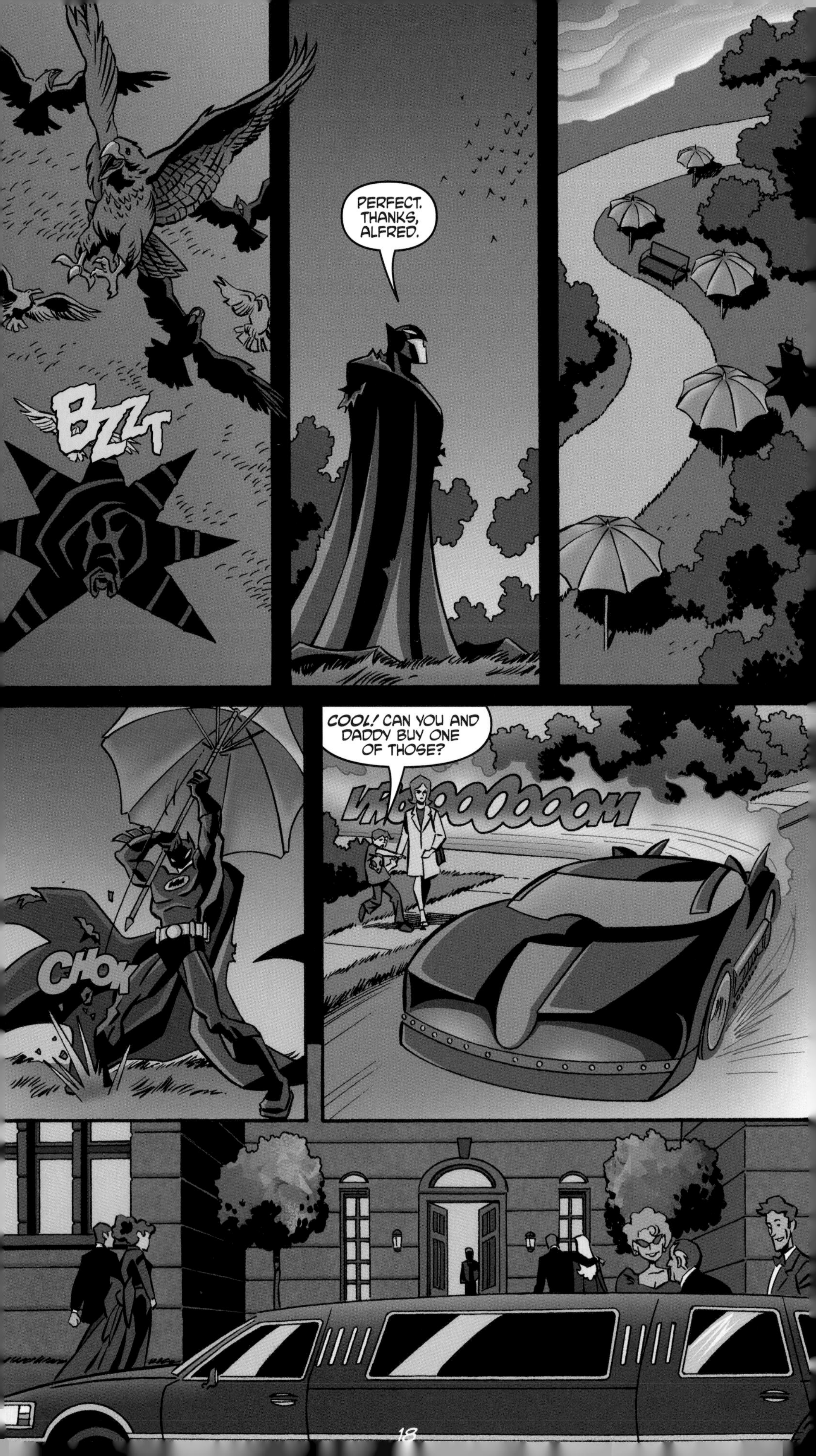
BZZT
PERFECT. THANKS, ALFRED.
CHOK
COOL! CAN YOU AND DADDY BUY ONE OF THOSE?
VROOOOOOOOM

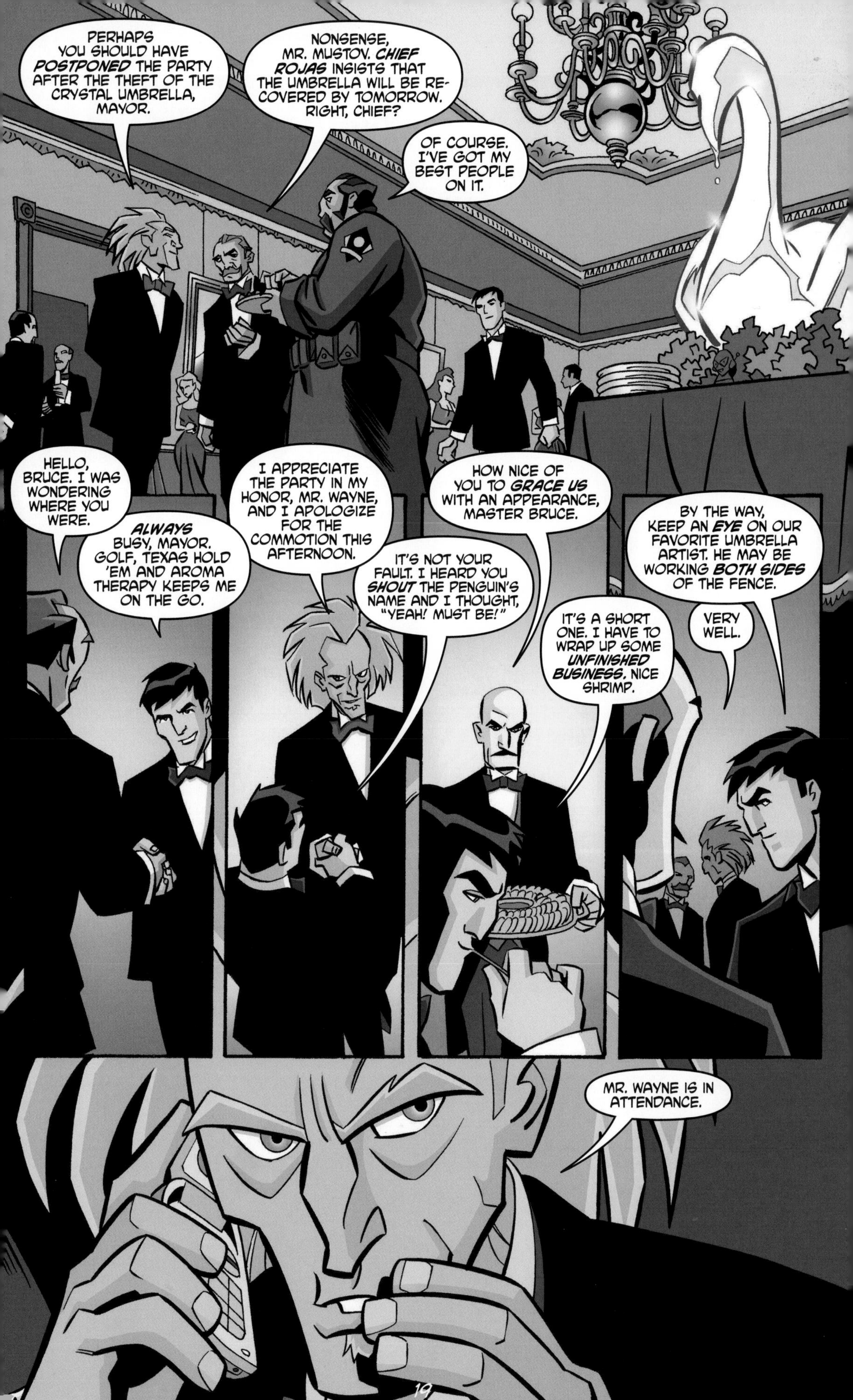
PERHAPS YOU SHOULD HAVE POSTPONED THE PARTY AFTER THE THEFT OF THE CRYSTAL UMBRELLA, MAYOR.
NONSENSE, MR. MUSTOV. CHIEF ROJAS INSISTS THAT THE UMBRELLA WILL BE RE-COVERED BY TOMORROW. RIGHT, CHIEF?
OF COURSE. I'VE GOT MY BEST PEOPLE ON IT.
HELLO, BRUCE. I WAS WONDERING WHERE YOU WERE.
ALWAYS BUSY, MAYOR. GOLF, TEXAS HOLD 'EM AND AROMA THERAPY KEEPS ME ON THE GO.
I APPRECIATE THE PARTY IN MY HONOR, MR. WAYNE, AND I APOLOGIZE FOR THE COMMOTION THIS AFTERNOON.
IT'S NOT YOUR FAULT. I HEARD YOU SHOUT THE PENGUIN'S NAME AND I THOUGHT, "YEAH! MUST BE!"
HOW NICE OF YOU TO GRACE US WITH AN APPEARANCE, MASTER BRUCE.
IT'S A SHORT ONE. I HAVE TO WRAP UP SOME UNFINISHED BUSINESS. NICE SHRIMP.
BY THE WAY, KEEP AN EYE ON OUR FAVORITE UMBRELLA ARTIST. HE MAY BE WORKING BOTH SIDES OF THE FENCE.
VERY WELL.
MR. WAYNE IS IN ATTENDANCE.

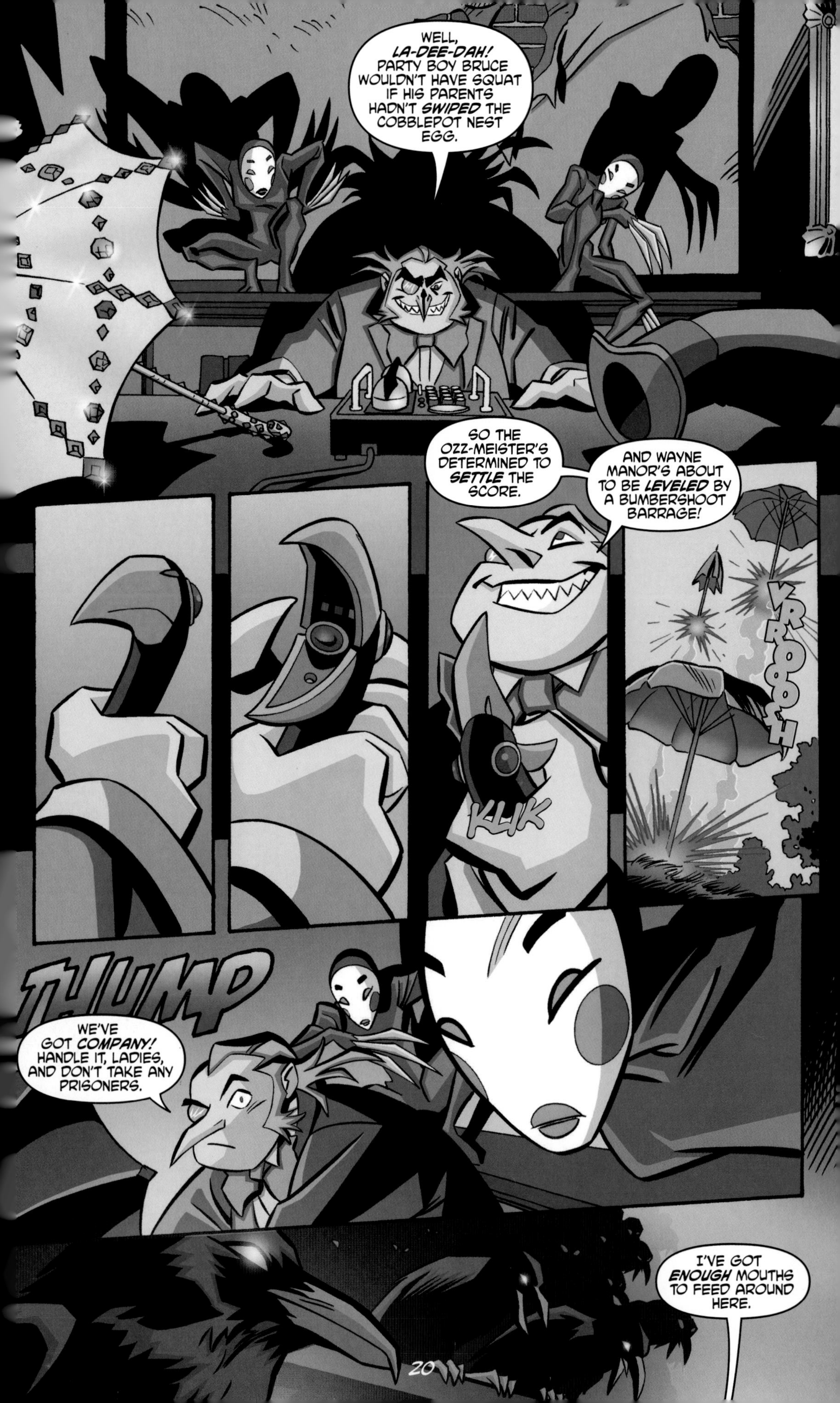
WELL, *LA-DEE-DAH!* PARTY BOY BRUCE WOULDN'T HAVE SQUAT IF HIS PARENTS HADN'T *SWIPED* THE COBBLEPOT NEST EGG.
SO THE OZZ-MEISTER'S DETERMINED TO *SETTLE* THE SCORE.
AND WAYNE MANOR'S ABOUT TO BE *LEVELED* BY A BUMBERSHOOT BARRAGE!
KLIK
VRROOOSH
THUMP
WE'VE GOT *COMPANY!* HANDLE IT, LADIES, AND DON'T TAKE ANY PRISONERS.
I'VE GOT *ENOUGH* MOUTHS TO FEED AROUND HERE.

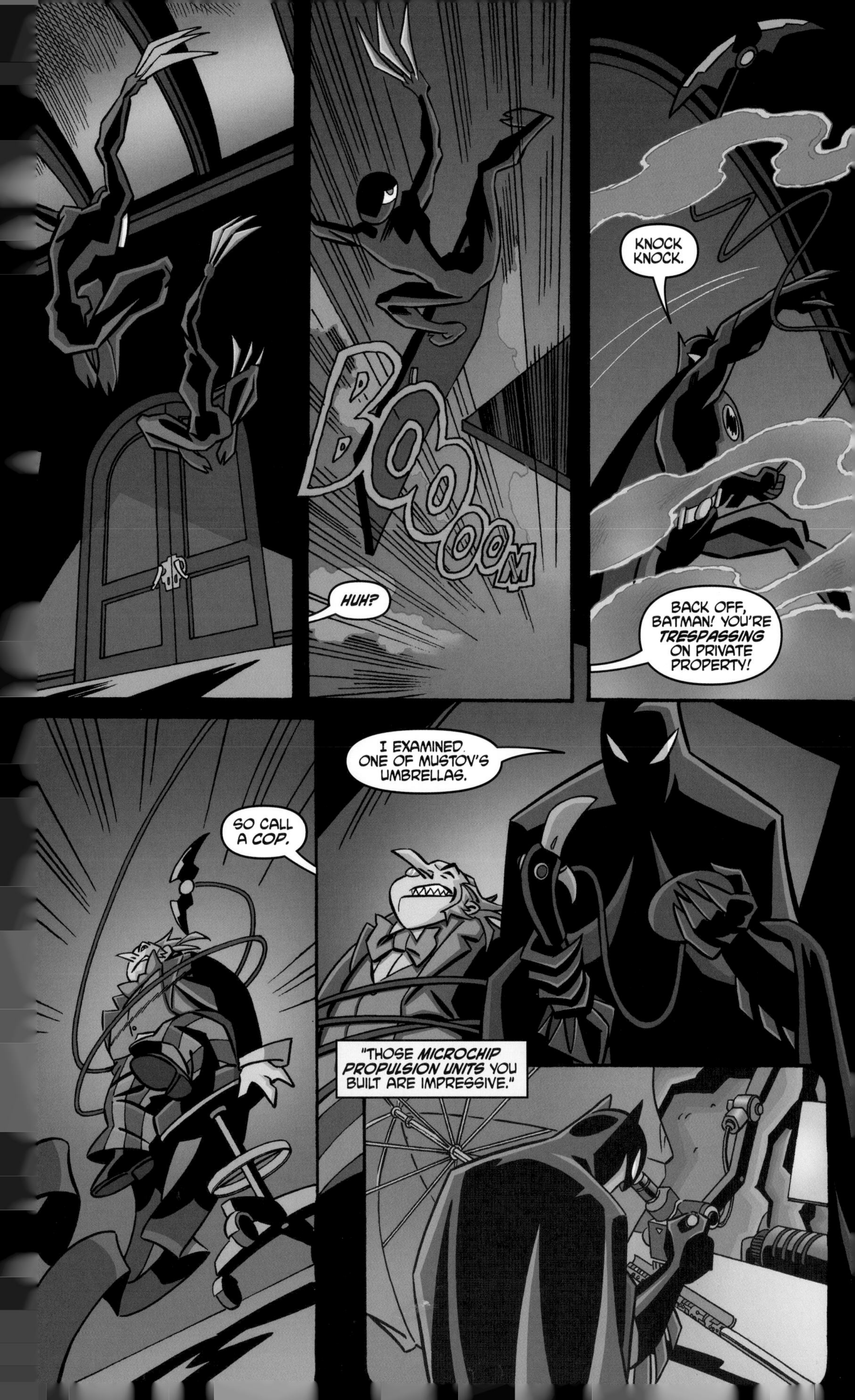
BOOOOOM
HUH?
KNOCK KNOCK.
BACK OFF, BATMAN! YOU'RE *TRESPASSING* ON PRIVATE PROPERTY!
SO CALL A *COP.*
I EXAMINED ONE OF MUSTOV'S UMBRELLAS.
"THOSE *MICROCHIP PROPULSION UNITS* YOU BUILT ARE IMPRESSIVE."

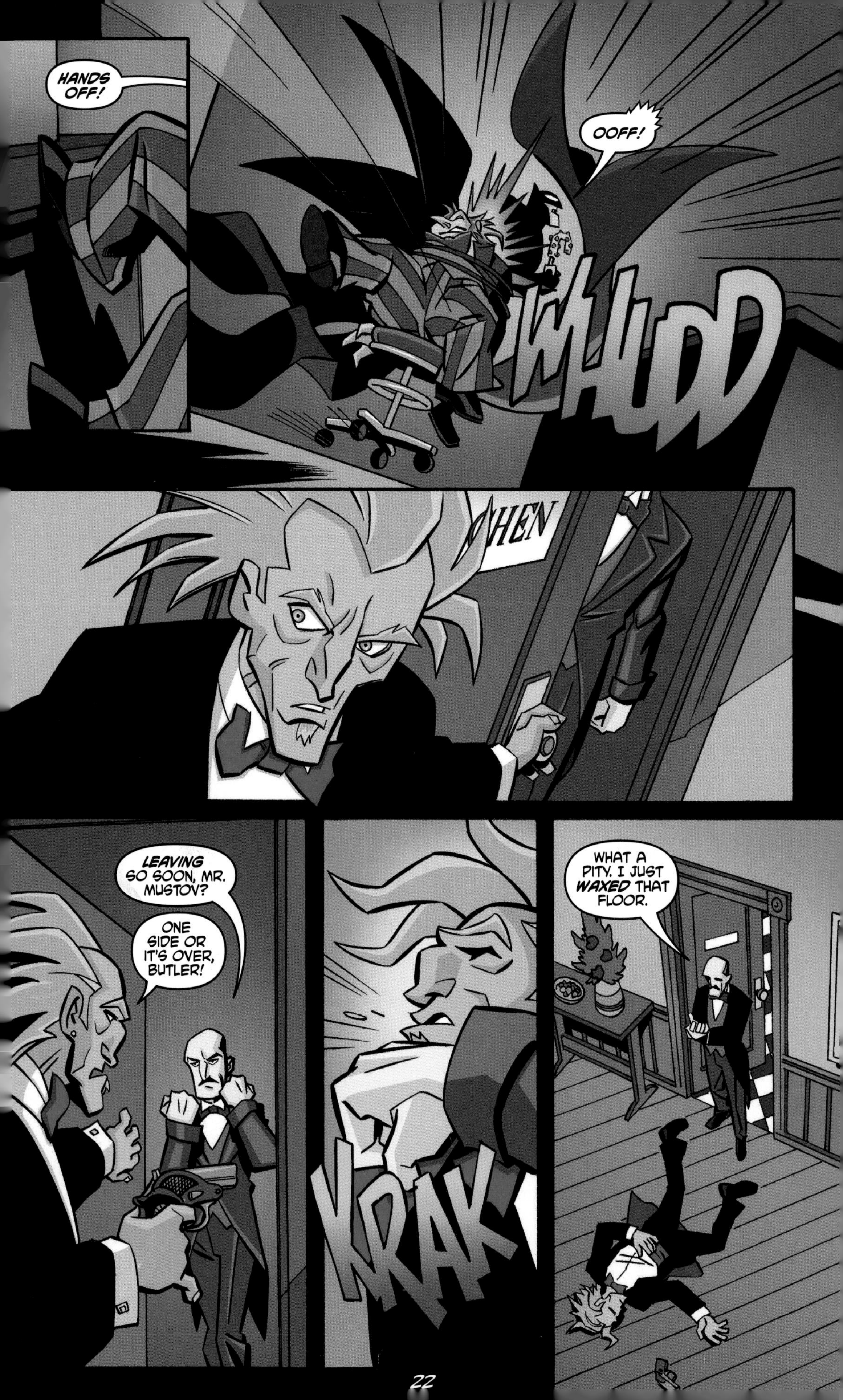
HANDS OFF!
OOFF!
WHUDD
WHEN
LEAVING SO SOON, MR. MUSTOV?
ONE SIDE OR IT'S OVER, BUTLER!
KRAK
WHAT A PITY. I JUST WAXED THAT FLOOR.

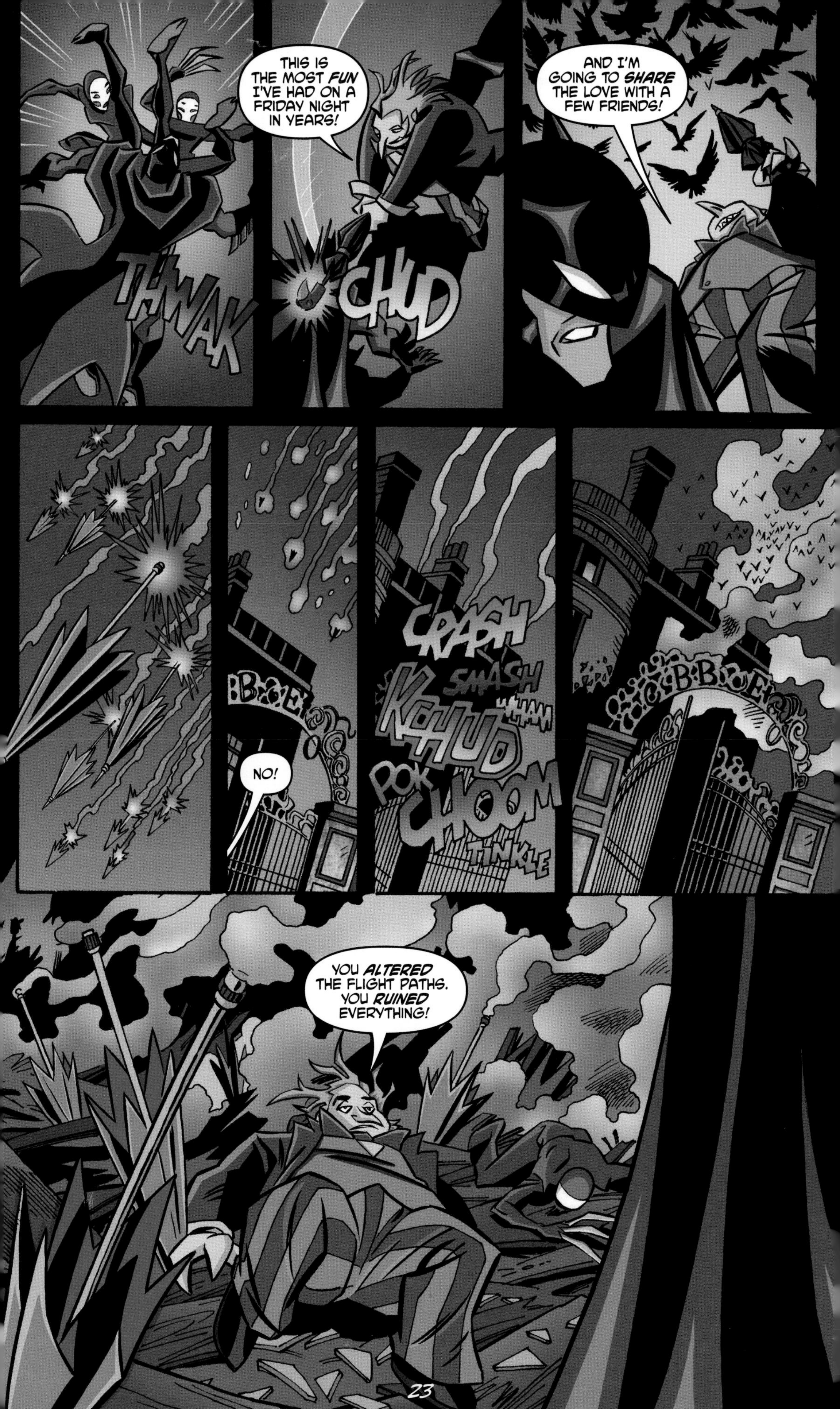
THWAK
THIS IS THE MOST FUN I'VE HAD ON A FRIDAY NIGHT IN YEARS!
CHUD
AND I'M GOING TO SHARE THE LOVE WITH A FEW FRIENDS!
NO!
CRASH
SMASH
WHAM
KACHUD
POK
CHOOM
TINKLE
YOU ALTERED THE FLIGHT PATHS. YOU RUINED EVERYTHING!

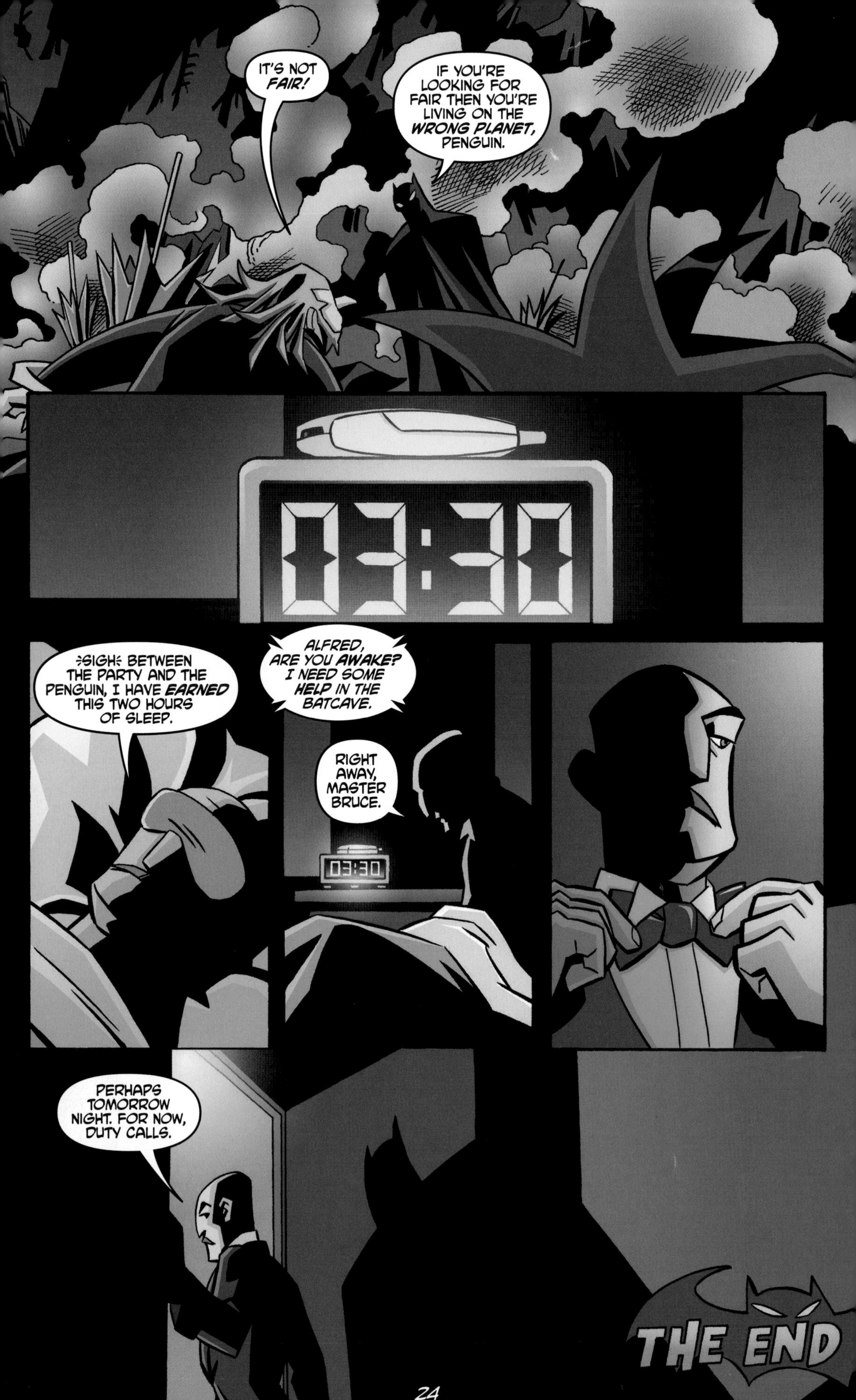
IT'S NOT *FAIR!*
IF YOU'RE LOOKING FOR FAIR THEN YOU'RE LIVING ON THE *WRONG PLANET,* PENGUIN.
03:30
⁂SIGH⁂ BETWEEN THE PARTY AND THE PENGUIN, I HAVE *EARNED* THIS TWO HOURS OF SLEEP.
ALFRED, ARE YOU AWAKE? I NEED SOME HELP IN THE BATCAVE.
RIGHT AWAY, MASTER BRUCE.
03:30
PERHAPS TOMORROW NIGHT. FOR NOW, DUTY CALLS.
THE END

CREATORS

BILL MATHENY WRITER
Along with comics like THE BATMAN STRIKES, Bill Matheny has written for TV series including KRYPTO THE SUPERDOG, WHERE'S WALDO, A PUP NAMED SCOOBY-DOO, and many others.

CHRISTOPHER JONES PENCILLER
Christopher Jones is an artist who has worked for DC Comics, Image, Malibu, Caliber, and Sundragon Comics.

TERRY BEATTY INKER
Terry Beatty has inked THE BATMAN STRIKES! and BATMAN: THE BRAVE AND THE BOLD as well as several other DC Comics graphic novels.

GLOSSARY

amplify (AM-pli-fye)--to make something louder or stronger

obligations (ahb-li-GAY-shuhns)--things you have to do

pecking order (PEK-ing ORR-dur)--a hierarchy based on status

postponed (pohst-POHND)--put something off until later

propulsion (pruh-PUHL-shuhn)--the force by which an object is pushed

souvenirs (soo-vuh-NEERZ)--objects that remind you of a certain person, place, or event

strategic (struh-TEE-jik)--clever or showing careful planning

sutures (SOO-churs)--strands used to sew together wounds on a living body

trespassing (TRES-pass-ing)--going onto private property without permission

variables (VAYR-ee-uh-buhls)--things that are likely to change

VISUAL QUESTIONS & PROMPTS

1. Why do you think the artists chose to place these panels side by side? How do the images work with the text to create the story?

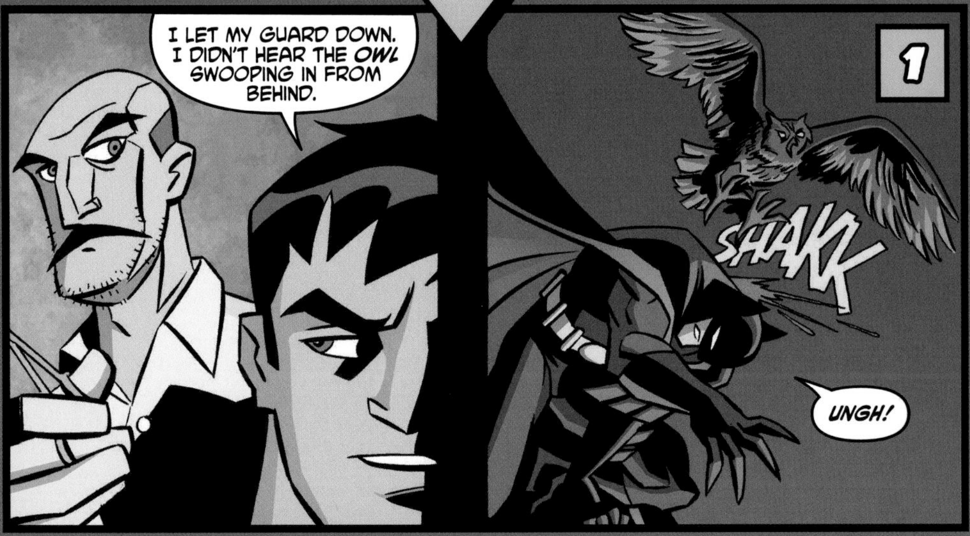
I LET MY GUARD DOWN. I DIDN'T HEAR THE *OWL* SWOOPING IN FROM BEHIND.
1
SHAKK
UNGH!

2. This is one panel, but it is broken up into several columns. What effect does that have on you as you read? What do you think the purpose is?

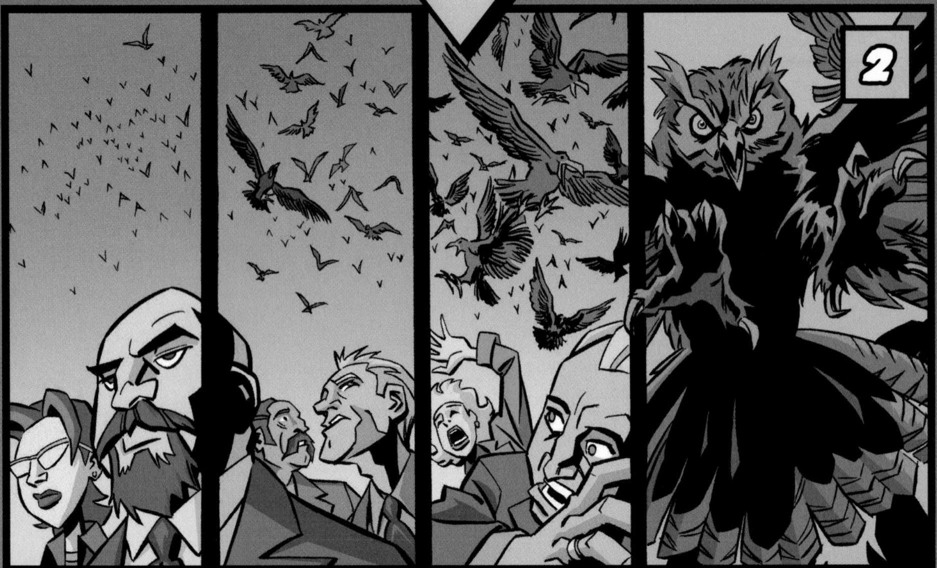
2

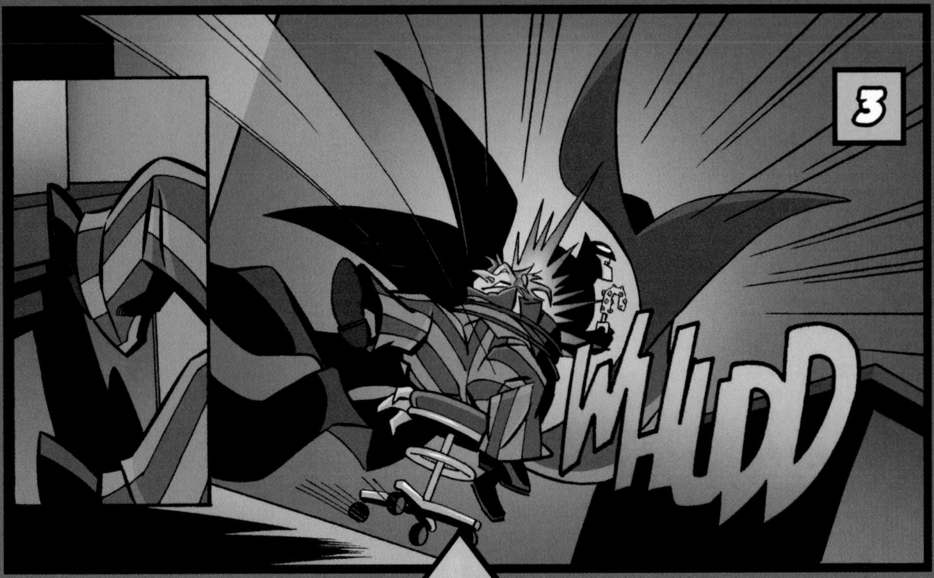
3
WHUDD

3. Why is there a separate panel zooming in on Cobblepot's foot? What do we learn from the close-up that we might not see otherwise?

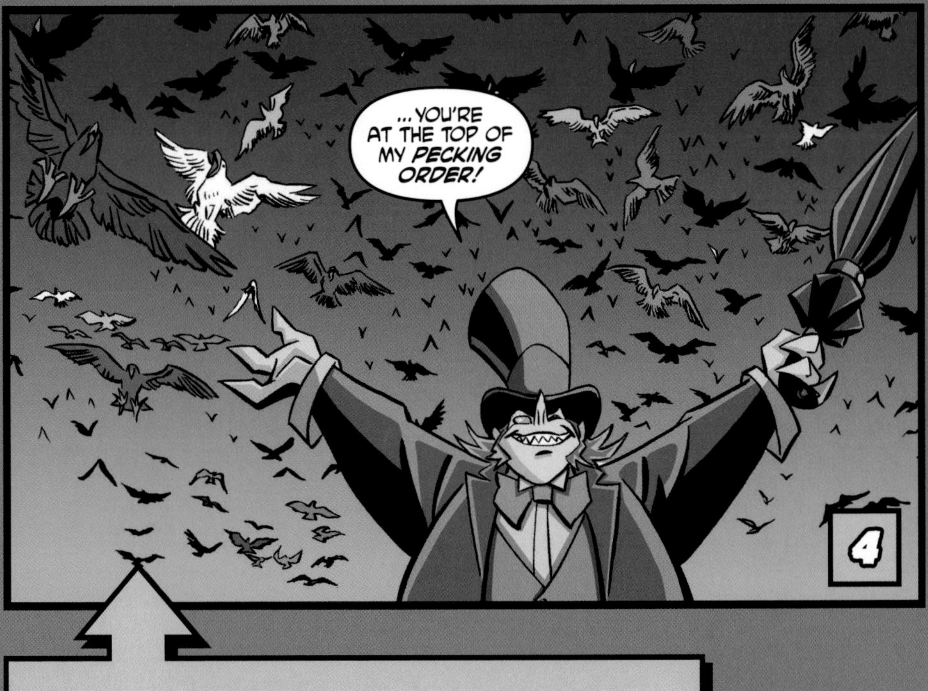
...YOU'RE AT THE TOP OF MY *PECKING ORDER!*
4

4. What's the double meaning behind Cobblepot's use of the phrase "pecking order"?

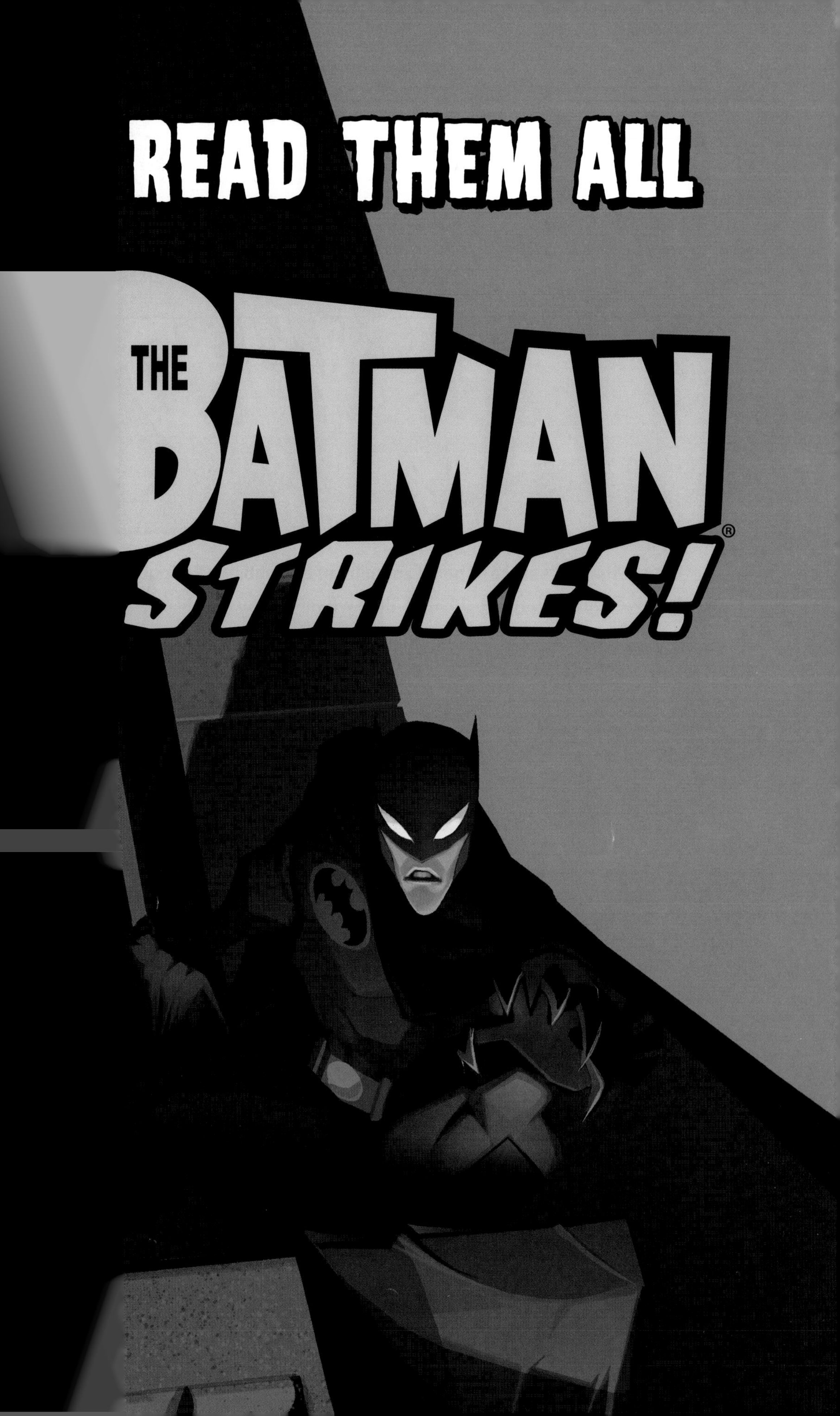
READ THEM ALL
THE BATMAN STRIKES!

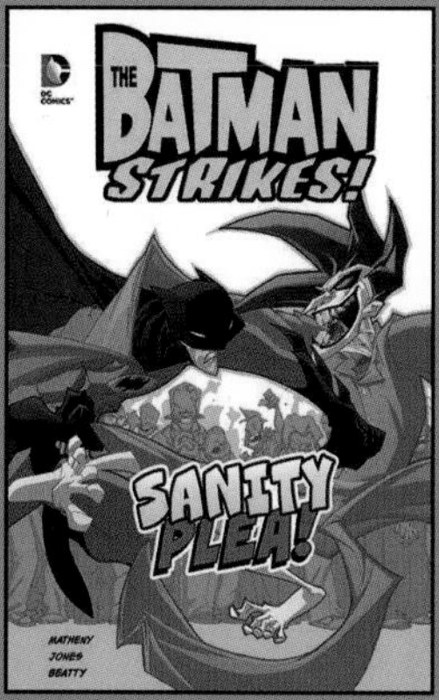

THE BATMAN STRIKES!
SANITY PLEA!
MATHENY
JONES
BEATTY

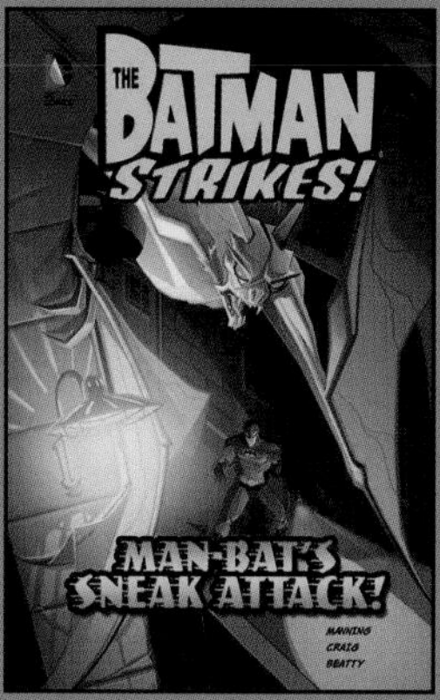

THE BATMAN STRIKES!
MAN-BAT'S SNEAK ATTACK!
MANNING
CRAIG
BEATTY

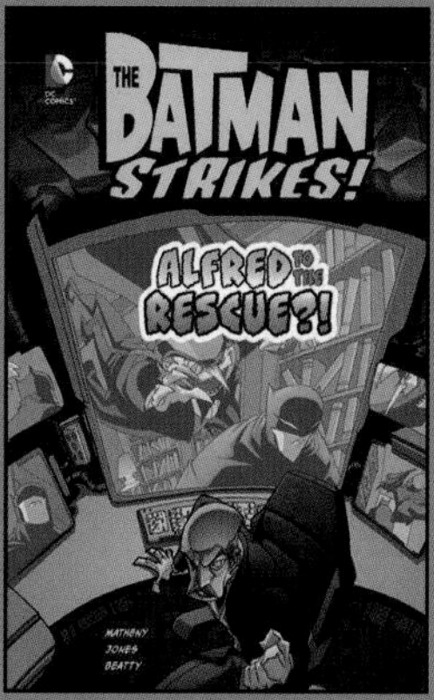

THE BATMAN STRIKES!
ALFRED TO THE RESCUE?!
MATHENY
JONES
BEATTY

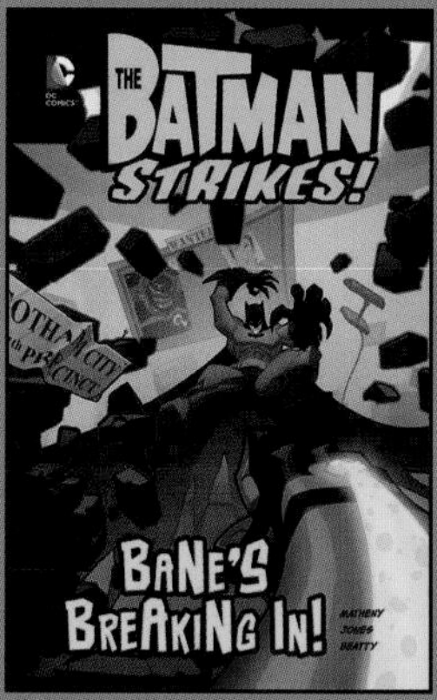

THE BATMAN STRIKES!
BANE'S BREAKING IN!
MATHENY
JONES
BEATTY

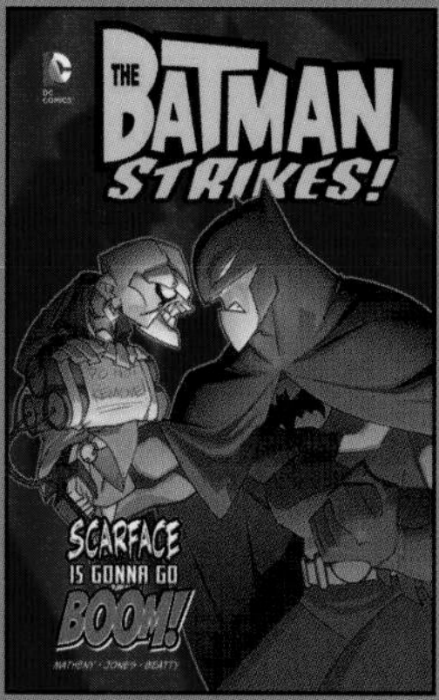

THE BATMAN STRIKES!
SCARFACE IS GONNA GO BOOM!
MATHENY · JONES · BEATTY

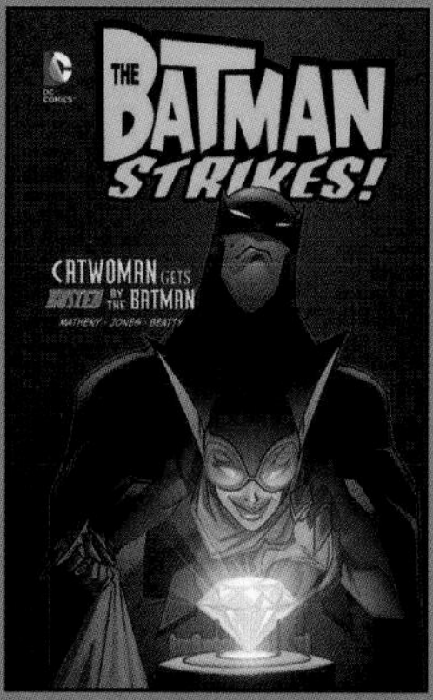

THE BATMAN STRIKES!
CATWOMAN GETS BUSTED BY THE BATMAN
MATHENY · JONES · BEATTY

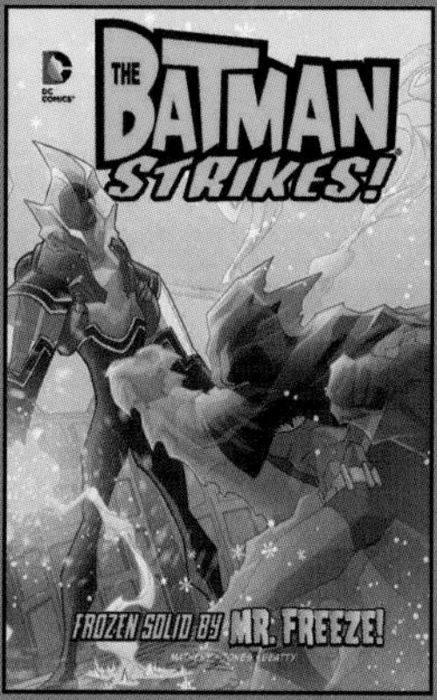

THE BATMAN STRIKES!
FROZEN SOLID BY MR. FREEZE!
MATHENY · JONES · BEATTY

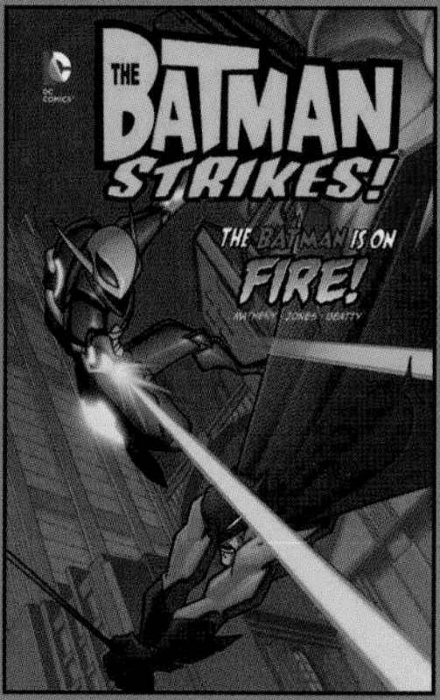

THE BATMAN STRIKES!
THE BATMAN IS ON FIRE!
MATHENY · JONES · BEATTY

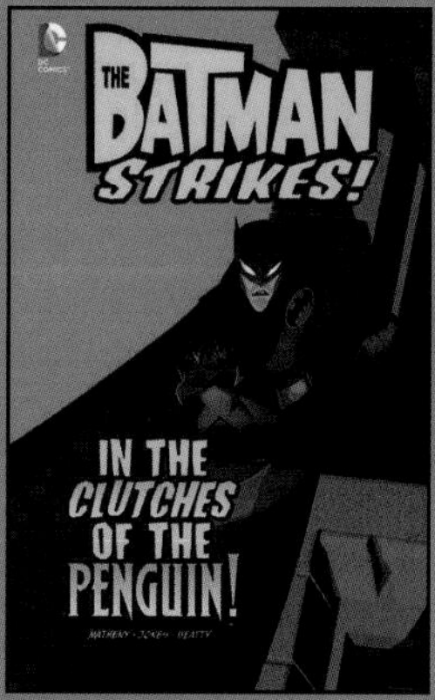

THE BATMAN STRIKES!
IN THE CLUTCHES OF THE PENGUIN!
MATHENY · JONES · BEATTY

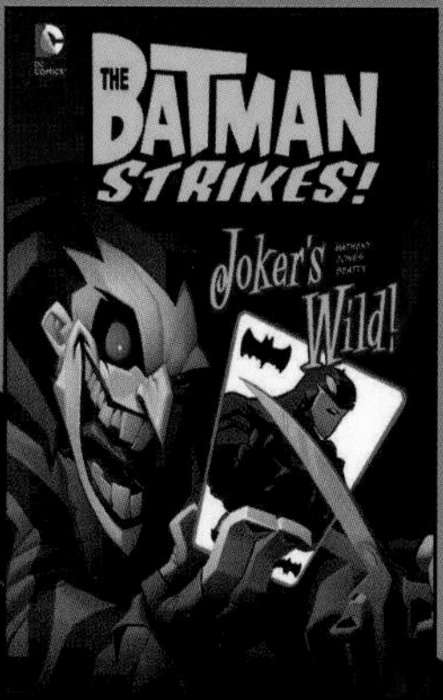

THE BATMAN STRIKES!
Joker's Wild!
MATHENY
JONES
BEATTY

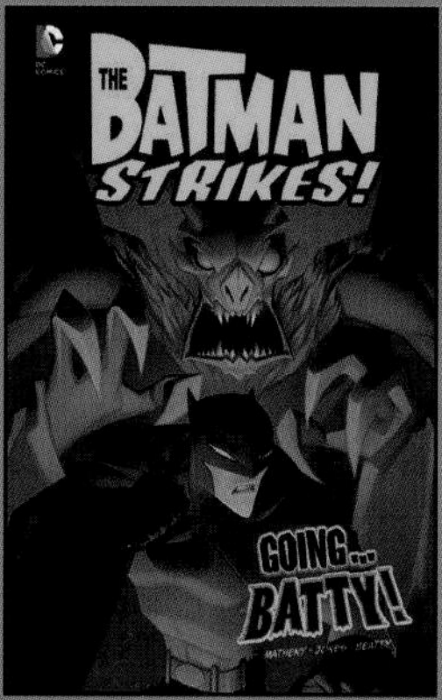

THE BATMAN STRIKES!
GOING... BATTY!
MATHENY · JONES · BEATTY

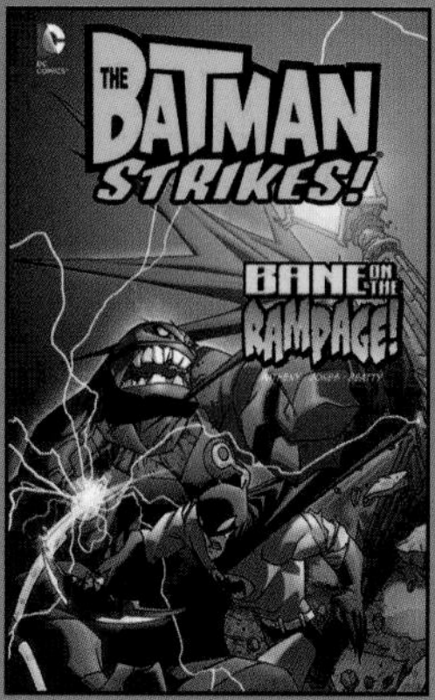

THE BATMAN STRIKES!
BANE ON THE RAMPAGE!
MATHENY · JONES · BEATTY

THE BATMAN STRIKES!®

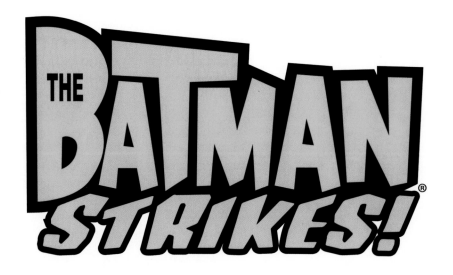

For Every
Individual...

The
INDIANAPOLIS PUBLIC
Library

Renew by Phone
269-5222

Renew on the Web
www.indypl.org

For General Library Information
please call 275-4100